*Praise for R. Conrad*

Speer is an original, both as a writer ... things others don't and writes with subtle, enticing power. He is a star in the making.

> ~ Lawrence Martin, author of ten books, with six national best sellers including *The Presidents and the Prime Ministers*, and journalist with *The Globe and Mail*.

Speer's wit and humour creates characters that are memorable and distinctive. Each tale is an absolute treasure. You won't put it down. *Saint Lazarus Day* is a must read!

> ~ Todd Devonshire, author of the novel *Rink Burgers* and several plays including the hit show *Monday Night*.

A welcome fresh voice in fiction. Speer's versatile style jumps smoothly within this range of deadpan and lyrical, realistic and absurd, with some stories being sort of deceptively simple yet larger disorienting tragicomedies at the same time. Impressive debut from Speer.

> ~ Dr. Robert Zubrin, author of the best-selling *The Case for Mars* and *The Case for Space*.

This is heartland Canada, with settings and engaging stories that remind you of home and lively characters which stay with you. Speer brings a fun and fresh pen to the national lit scene, exploring the human experience, as flawed and outrageous as it often is.

> ~ Russell Hillier, author of *Pawns of War* and the Canadian best seller *One Soldier*.

# Saint Lazarus Day

## *and Other Stories*

## R. CONRAD SPEER

*atmosphere press*

*To C.E. and G.W.*

# CONTENTS

# Woodpeckers of Triangulum

On finishing our brunch in town, we drove for about an hour down towards the river valley. We parked next to the base of an abandoned train trestle and had been walking for several hours—we'd been following official hiking routes along the river at the outset and for the most part, until we took a turn off the beaten path sometime in the late afternoon. I didn't pay too much attention, as I was following the lead of my friend Tom, who said he knew precisely where he was going.

It was supposed to be a more or less casual hike we were going on, on the pleasant Saturday afternoon that it was, but he wanted to break script with a minor detour, as he was planning to guide the two of us over to a swampy section of dead trees where he claimed there was no better spot to view several different species of woodpeckers, all living there together in what sounded as though it was some sort of Disney-like harmony. I thought it would be a nice deviation from the worn routes or even a good purpose of the nature walk, so I followed Tom, the would-be tour guide and amateur ornithologist, off of the well-manicured main trails and down into the dense woods of the river valley.

"There was a major fire down there a few years ago," said Tom, as he carefully pushed away a series of willow branches in his path, kindly ensuring they wouldn't snap back and whip me. "There are lots of lush grasses and fresh flowers on the forest floor—clover and fireweed and so on. They have grown back quite nicely, but many of the charred trees right there are still quite dead. And that is what the woodpeckers really love, as they can move straight into the hollowed-out cavities and live there, in those burnt out tree trunks, a morbid sort of home sweet home for them."

Tom had the air about him as if he was a professor in the specialty of whatever he was talking about at the given moment, whether actual academic topics or otherwise, giving off this vibe as he transformed the minutiae into significant and grand. While oxymoronically fascinating and mundane, it was invariably quirky—notwithstanding my own mood on each certain occasion probably being a contributing factor to how I viewed the words of Tom. Sometimes it was clear he was an authority on the subject, for whatever reason that came about. But as often as not, it seemed like rubbish, and whether he knew it or didn't know, whether he was playing one intentionally or just making up some random shit in his own special world, devil's advocate also had to be played, at a minimum—if not an explicit calling out of his reeking bull. As we'd been buds since college and continued to grow or at least extend the relationship through time, I had no trouble whatsoever in hitting him back on any of those fronts, as needed, whether it was for the real education or only a bit of playful entertainment, gentle and harmless.

"When was the last time you were out here, searching for your birds?" I said, interested in seeing the burnt trees and possibly the woodpeckers, but I was now starting to get whipped by the odd errant willow branch, while scratching my bare legs against other questionable evergreen flora as we walked further afield, deeper into the bush growing thick along the slopes of the valley.

"I was here about this time last summer, right around the solstice," said Tom, trudging forward and working the brush like an explorer, looking as though he was longing for a machete to clear a new path in the virgin jungle ahead. "It was only the one time. It is funny, as I found it by accident. I was only looking for some chanterelles and herbs, and I stumbled upon the blackened tract in a happy encounter. In that sanctuary of a dead and boggy zone, there were eight different species of woodpeckers I saw in under an hour, including a couple you rarely ever see around here. Simply amazing and, I imagine, almost unprecedented."

"And so, did you get your mushrooms and whatnot then, or you just got to see those different peckers, all living together in peace?" I said, walking behind sessional lecturer-trailblazer Tom, trying to follow his steps of the newly trampled corridor he was creating, while moving forward like a feinting boxer or a limbo-dancer to avoid the elastic branches coming at me on the rebound.

"Heh, only the woodpeckers," said Tom, offering a light laugh as he began to slow his pace. "I was fascinated, so I started taking pictures and before I knew it, it was getting dark out and I needed to find my way out, back to the main trails again. It is quite a sight to see, and a perfect early summer day for it, so I do hope we get to see them all again, or at least a few of them, the more interesting ones."

"Remind me, what are they all called again?" I said, feeding Tom's excitement of the prospect. "And which are the rare ones?"

"Right, so there are the Hairy, the Downy, the Pileated, the Red-headed, the American Three-toed, the Black-backed, the Yellow-bellied Sapsucker, and the Northern Flicker," said Tom, with a gesture of concrete authority on this specific subject, even counting them off on each finger, one-by-one, as if he were still in kindergarten. "The Red-headed you do not normally see because it is out of their range around here. The American Three-toed you quite simply do not usually see at all; if you are to see them on those rare and magical occasions, they are more common in these types of woodlot areas with the dead trees, as it is easier living in there. The others are all more common birds, to varying degrees. Here is hoping we have timed our visit right—I do believe we might have."

"Which one is the Woody Woodpecker one or are we going to get to see him at all?" I said, as I wanted to go along with it at least a bit, reminding Tom that I was sort of interested in his insightful knowledge on some level, but also with the tone that I didn't really care about this silliness either way.

"Yes, he is a Pileated Woodpecker, and I did see him there last year," Tom said, serious but still quite excited. "He is the one with the bright red crest all about the top of his head—and as large as a good-sized crow, if not quite the size of a raven. They are huge birds and look rather exotic, as if they should be living in the tropics somewhere, with the macaws and toucans, not here with our bland sparrows and wrens."

"The punk rocker pecker," I said, trying to parrot Tom's enthusiasm. "Good stuff, let's go see him then. How far to go now, do you figure?"

I tried to look through and past him, but it was only thick brush surrounding us. Being so close to the river, there were no particularly huge trees around, rather it was crowded with shrubs, bushes, and the like—willows, caraganas, switchgrass, quackgrass, thistles, and other thorny plants. If he had taken a dozen steps forward without me, I wouldn't have been able to see him, even with him wearing his ridiculous and out-of-season neon apricot hunter's ballcap. *Safety first, good for Tom,* I thought. It was even more silly in that he wasn't a hunter to begin with—not that he didn't like the idea of hunting in theory, which he did, but he didn't practice it himself, aside from wearing his inane hat. Tom was more of a gatherer type of fellow. I had always thought that he was also a follower type, although here he was leading me around—ushering us off the main path and I was now beginning to wonder, *To where, exactly, is he taking us?*

"We are not too far away now, although I think we might be slightly off of our course, if only a smidgeon perhaps," said Tom, pausing for a rest with his hands on his hips, and to seemingly gather his bearings. "I think we need to direct ourselves up a bit towards those elms and poplars over there, as we are still too low, too close to the river down here."

I couldn't understand how he'd be able to figure that out based on where we currently were, stuck in the middle of this thick brush somewhere in the valley, now a good couple of hours off the main (and well-mapped) hiking trails. I was also at the point of not getting why he would have wandered so far off last year on his mushroom-picking adventure, and I was starting to disbelieve it. I was thinking: I could believe that he did it in terms of randomly leaving the path in pursuit of his beloved chanterelles, but at this point in our hike I wasn't any longer convinced that this was in fact the route he'd chosen a year ago; and, even if it was, he now had no clue where we were in relation to that past effort. Part of me was wanting to go ahead of Tom and lead the way, letting the willow branches fly, whipping him good as punishment for piloting us astray.

"Sounds good, let's climb," I said, wanting to move out of our present quagmire and onto some friendlier terrain up above, hopefully keeping our spirits up with respect to both the end goal and the basic direction of the walk. "So how do you know the difference between each type of bird, especially since some look so similar—not to mention the sexes of the same kind are even a bit different, so how do you spot the nuance? It's probably not unlike your selection of forest floor mushrooms, where lookalikes are indeed quite a different species?"

"Great question, and yes, mushrooms are somewhat analogous, to be sure—a missed nuance with respect to fungal growth can even be fatal," said Tom, as he focused on the new direction of the hike as well as this question of detail on which he so thrived. "It is the look, mostly. The sex thing is not as important, or I should say it is ultimately pretty easy to distinguish the male and female of a given species of bird, once you know that type of woodpecker well enough, where there is a more defined colour here or there, a slightly different pattern on the male, that sort of thing. But you are right, and the Downy versus the Hairy is a perfect example of what you are asking about. The Hairy is only marginally larger, a bit longer beak, some minor variation in speckled patterns on their tail feathers compared to the Downy—maybe some inconsistent temperament and other behaviours here and there, but they look a lot alike: near doppelgängers is the bottom line. It is the same between the American Three-toed and the Black-backed—they are almost identical twins, with the same mustard streak on their heads, with the only visible difference being the black back of the Black-backed, rather than some speckles on his counterpart, as I think even it has three toes just like the Three-toed one. I would have to check my trusty bird book at home..."

Tom continued on with his detailed explanations of each kind of woodpecker (becoming more ridiculous each time as his explanations offered an even greater level of detail) until we came to the taller trees we'd recently viewed from afar; however, on reaching them, we realized it was only an illusion that they were on higher ground and somewhat out of the lower part of the valley. In fact, rather than on a slope, the trees appeared to be on even lower ground, with the soil becoming sandier and damper at their base, evidently near some major recent moisture incident, whether a late spring melt or run-off, or a heavy rain with localized flooding that may have caused some pooling here.

It had been many hours since we had set out on the main path. The sun was going down, with dusk in motion, the western sky transforming from the day-long and systemic dazzling cobalt to the strokes of lighter ambers and red ochres, with darker navies and purples following closely behind. A spring flowed towards and almost through the trees, winding tightly around them with a good trickle. We filled our empty bottles with the clean water, looking in each direction of the flow, knowing it was ultimately headed into the river, and assuming it was emerging from a hill or at least a possible source of some higher ground, maybe.

I knew full well we were now hopelessly lost, and Tom also gave up the charade to admit as much. While my thoughts were turning from light willow whips to solid birch clubs, I knew there was no point in either of us getting too upset or pointing to the obvious source of this inevitable tragicomedy unfolding—no, I needn't lay the blame on Tom; not now, anyway. We quickly agreed it made sense with limited and fading daylight to get out of the near riverbed we were standing in under the once promising poplar tree. We agreed we should try to hug the bank of the little spring, believing it would be the least obstructive path through the silty forest floor here in the valley, as it would ideally lead us up a hill of some sort for a greater view of our surroundings, terrain, and the river, if not even pinpoint our precise location somehow.

"Why isn't that sapsucker or flicker bird called a woodpecker like all the others?" I said, trying to use an encouraging tone so Tom would continue onward and not worry about our current predicament of his own making. "And they eat seeds and suet and whatnot like the others, or is it just sap from trees for the eponymous bird, that sucker pecker one?"

"Yes, they all love the backyard suet, if they can get their beaks on it," said Tom, picking up his pace as if to make up for lost time. "Nuts, seeds, fruit. That sapsucker likes the sap, for sure, but they do not actually suck it. It's more like they lick it like an ice cream cone, or they lap it up like a cat does with its water or cream. They drill holes when pecking, making compact wells almost, which makes the sap run out—they eat that, and also the bugs and larvae that flow out of the tree with the sap. And flickers like flies, ants, grubs, that sort of thing. There are even some woodpeckers strong enough to take out smaller birds and rodents, like a bird of prey—a hawk or falcon or something."

"The mighty woodpecker, the unknown big game hunter, the carnivore killer," I said, not wanting to mock or be an overt jackass, but rather bridge the conversation elsewhere, out of interest in a new forthcoming topic, or bored with the current trajectory, and also trying to push the limits of Tom's knowledge, whether legitimate or phony. "How do they stay vertical on trees like that? You'd think they'd slip and fall off. And what about the jackhammering away at wood—don't they get a kind of sawdust or something in their eyes and down in their lungs, choking the little peckers out?"

"Those are great questions, certainly," said Tom, keen to answer appropriately, even if he offered a mild breath of condescension in the response. Tom knew I was not thrilled with the status of our hike. "Their tail feathers are so strong they can brace themselves against trees and poles, holding themselves up and digging in their tiny talons on their toes, like ice-climbing boots with steel picks, clutching on. They can filter out that sawdust material with their nose feathers, like a 3M furnace filter. Woodpeckers are almost like robots, with iron-like skulls, tough-as-nails necks and bills for all that jackhammering, Terminator birds. They peck away to find a mate, as if the louder and harder they peck makes a good mate, but also for the more utilitarian purpose of finding stuff to eat, sometimes even listening into the wood first to track down the bug before drilling it out, like a fox listening to mice rustling under the snow..."

The next good hour went by like this, on and on—trivia on the fauna (solely woodpeckers), but also on the flora (poplar this, juniper that; chokecherry this, dogwood that). It was an idle and ludicrous conversation about what now seemed like mythical birds, as if the woodpeckers were dodos or even pterodactyls, never to be seen outside a museum again. We were only trying to take our minds away from the current struggle of a walk, as we were totally lost in the forest, now in complete darkness with nightfall having arrived on the banks of our meandering brook, an invisible trickle somewhere in the immediate proximity of our feet. "We'll have to find a spot to stop and rest or we're going to walk into a hole or off a cliff or something," I said, having stumbled and tripped a couple of times each and every minute for the past twenty or so minutes. "I can't keep going over these roots and rocks in the dark, let alone trying to get through this thick brush any longer. I think it's game over for tonight."

"Fair point, for sure," said Tom, conceding we were not just lost, but also that we were not going to go any further today in this dark forest. "We will find our way back down to the river at dawn and we can walk out that way, as our precise whereabouts will be known at that time. Or better yet, maybe there is a high enough elevation around here and then we will have a good and complete picture of where we are, a perfect bird's-eye view. Sunrise is only a few hours away..."

It was only meant to be a short afternoon hike, but with the tail end of dusk having been a couple of hours ago already, I assumed it must have been after midnight when we gave up on the futile return effort, which my watch confirmed for me. We sat down on a clear space of open bluff, as it had a meadow-like grassy cover, which felt dry enough, and without anything that might fall on us from directly above during the night, save for maybe something like owl poo; I had my doubts that errant bird shit would rain down on us in the night from any of Tom's fabled woodpeckers around here. While it was getting quite late, both the time and our frustration and disappointment with the whole scenario meant we wouldn't really be sleeping tonight, only resting till our blindness was cured at dawn.

I took my water bottle out of my backpack, sort of fluffed the bag, setting it down to lie properly and have a good rest while I could and while I had absolutely nothing else to do. Tom quickly followed suit, lying parallel and giving about two feet of free space between us. One couldn't quite see the moon from our position, but there were innumerable visible stars straight above us on this clear and now pitch-dark summer night.

"Look at that," said Tom, excited by something so much so that he propped himself right back up into a normal sitting position, feverishly taking out his bird-watching binoculars for verification. "We might not have been able to see all those goddamn woodpeckers, but look at that. That is Andromeda, the large bright spot. It is spiral-shaped, which we could see if we had brought along my telescope. And—wait one minute...yes, unbelievable! Sure as shit, there is Triangulum, the smaller one, the fainter speckle just below it. That one looks like a child's pinwheel—again, through some magnification, if we had it with us. Amazing!"

"What are those, stars or something?" I said, genuinely ignorant of space and sky-gazing. Hell, I didn't know my woodpeckers, I didn't know my mushrooms (only learning of chanterelles from an earlier story and related dinner hosted by Tom), and beyond knowing that the moon was indeed the moon, I thought about space, *Forget it and never mind if it has anything to do with the larger universe.*

"They look like stars, in their constellations up there," said Tom, his excitement racing with this great find from his naked eye, confirmed by his binocs, and so much further away than a woodpecker perched in a dead tree right in front of him here on this local and earthly ground. "But those are actually two different and individual galaxies, our nearest neighbouring galaxies, in fact."

It seemed unlikely he would know that level of detail concerning stars and their constellations, let alone positions of abstract galaxies. But yet again he gave off his authentic vibe of certainty that only Tom could, perhaps merely fabricating it in attempting some sort of redemption from the disastrously failed birding expedition we were still on, sitting on this moss and clover patch by a creek we couldn't even see right in front of us.

"Our solar system—we are in the Milky Way galaxy here," said Tom, knowing I was completely lost with his space talk, not just lost in the woods down here on planet Earth. He handed me his binoculars and began adjusting my position, helping me as to where exactly I should be looking in the night sky, and what I should be looking for—the brighter one first and then channeling my angle of sight over to the other one. "In ours and those two other galaxies, there are hundreds of billions of stars right here in our immediate galactic neighbourhood, which can only mean there must be many trillions of planets, just in our own Virgo supercluster here, not to mention the entire observable universe. Sagan said, 'We live on an insignificant planet of a humdrum star lost in a galaxy tucked away in some forgotten corner of a universe.' I think he meant both us and our peckers."

"Heh, it is truly amazing," I said, biting at his decent attempt at humour and allowing him to redeem himself a bit, as there was no benefit to our situation in souring the mood further, and truth be told, all of those planets and stars in the galaxy and universe really was an unquestionably awesome thought. "Surreal, really. Incomprehensible."

I considered asking him about how the sea-faring explorers of hundreds of years ago used the stars and constellations as maps to guide them around the land and the sea without becoming disoriented. It would have been a relevance so powerful that it couldn't possibly have been lost on him here tonight in our quandary; but, I decided against it, preferring to simply look up into space in great wonder, and in relative peace and quiet, even if bird-free.

"It is incredible, and the odds are pretty good that on one or more of those trillions of planets, they have forms of life with some close level of a parallel resemblance to here on Earth, if not an identical carbon copy. If you cast an objective eye on the science of it all, it would be arrogant and naïve to think otherwise," said Tom, still beyond excited, sounding as if he was still quoting Sagan or some other astronomer, yet he was calming himself down and with a more philosophical and quite serious tone. "And so, I would say that some of those planets way out there, revolving around their stars—they most probably even have something like their own woodpeckers, just like our own woodpeckers right down here."

# The Collar

Bobby had been dominating the calf roping circuit all season, winning at the past three rodeos—all mere warm-up acts for the championship event in his hometown this coming weekend.

"That's how you do it, like that," said Bobby, sitting atop his horse, yanking the rope just enough to make the umber calf bawl.

Bobby was showing the calf who was boss. As he pulled the noose tighter, a light rain fell in the pen, dampening the surface of the dirt on the cool, mid-summer morning day. The other cattle huddled in terror at the opposite end of the corral, as if they were safe in numbers and protecting one another, yet defenseless from the inevitable rope.

"All in the timing, the anticipation of its move?" Zane said. Bobby's younger cousin sat on the corral fence watching Bobby jerk the rope again. Zane, the novice, twirled his own rope down around his dusty boots, dangling his feet during this informal lassoing lesson.

The corral was at the end of a pasture. A crow quarreled with a magpie on the steel gate, then flew into a slender jack pine a few feet beyond the farmyard road. The road cut a path between the corral and the edge of the forest. A thick alpine woodland of evergreens stood as a lush wall beyond the first row of trees—a dense wilderness of life in the foothills, at the base of the mountains.

"Based on your position, how fast you're movin', how fast the calf moves," said Bobby. "What's its next move gonna be? You've got to be able to read that, like any play on the field, but out there in the dirt...in front of the lovely ladies sittin' in the grandstand, the wannabe cowgirls."

The ridgeback at Zane's side stood up and began barking, out of character for the dog. Zane figured the dog might have been disturbed by the growing frenzy of scavenger birds squawking above. The birds took short flights between trees, advancing to higher branches on each flutter, as if chasing one another up.

The heeler left Bobby's side, abandoning the hard but fun work of nipping the cattle in the corral to stand next to his canine colleague. The heeler looked between Bobby and Zane, and the woods.

"Do you find it better to know you've got it secured before jumping off, or are you comfortable enough feeling or knowing you're going to lasso it, you know, based on how close you are, and both of your speeds?" Zane said, trying to absorb the valuable knowledge from his seasoned cousin, Bobby, the one with all the rodeo hardware, the experience.

The sentinel dogs both stood at determined attention and barked. The ridgeback stayed at Zane's side by the fence, to warn and defend; the heeler ran back to Bobby, who was still on his horse, the dog circling him and the black stallion, obvious anxiety abounding in his bark.

"Sometimes I'd like to rope this mutt here and do more than just choke him a bunch," said Bobby, frowning at the dog as if that meant something to it.

Zane laughed and looked down to the ridgeback, the dog now grunting, flexing, frothing, and concentrating on the forest. Zane followed the dog's eyes, leaning down to more accurately see the dog's point of view. Together, they saw the black bear come running out of the woods, on a direct path towards the corral.

"Oh, shit!" Zane said, yelling and jumping up to stand on the highest rung of the fence, ensuring the dog remained below as his last line of defense.

The bear ran out of the trees, across the dirt road, and straight into the open gate of the corral, as if seeking its own comfort in numbers with the cows—or more likely an easy, quick meal of beef, if not quite veal any longer. The bear was realizing the mistake, turning left, turning right, and standing up on its hind legs to get a better view of these new surroundings. The bear was stunned as it looked at the herd and Bobby for a couple of seconds, then turned around and ran back out the gate, as fast as it had entered. The cattle were restless, bawling and lowing, pushing and rocking the fence, looking for an escape wherever they might be lucky enough to find one, as if they might stumble into a worm hole or at least bust out.

On horseback, Bobby got a good look from above when it ran in and then ran back out. Realizing it was only a small bear (a black bear, and while not a spring cub, not a large male either), he gave chase on the horse with his free rope released from the calf, galloping full-on ahead and cowboy-style, as if in a scene from a vintage western movie. The horse was nervous, but trusted Bobby.

Knowing what Bobby was doing and relying on his cousin's judgment to alleviate his own personal fears, Zane pivoted to the other side of the corral fence, planning to head off and corner the bear on the road, or send it back home into the woods.

"Zane!" said Bobby, screaming and pointing as he rode, knowing exactly which direction the bear would flee.

The bear avoided the forest and made an inadvertent beeline straight for Zane, as it appeared to be the only passage out: down the road, away from the woods, and towards the farmhouse. Zane relaxed and focused, taking a deep breath in as if he was about to pull a trigger. He let his rope go. When the bear stood up, the success was clear, as the lasso had landed perfectly over the bear's head, raised paws, and around its torso. Zane tugged hard on the rope to cinch it as tight as he could, while continuing to stand on the outer rungs of the fence, in position to jump back to the inside safe side of the corral, if things went sideways.

His grip on the noose was loose. The bear kept running to avoid the dogs, ripping the rope right out of Zane's hands, then climbing up a lone and scraggly pine between the road and corral. The cousins met at the base of the pallid tree, one on foot and one on horse.

The bear made its way twenty or so feet up the tree, positioning itself on a clean branch to view the danger below. The end of the rope hung down to within easy reach of grabbing it, like a leash. Bobby disembarked to join Zane on the ground, leaving his own calf roping rope on the saddle of the horse, leaving the horse standing by the fence, neighing, snorting, and kicking.

"Honour's all yours," said Bobby, taking the rope and passing it to Zane, smiling. "You gonna pull your new pet bear on down then?"

Zane took the reins. The loyal dogs barked up the tree and back towards the forest, rotating their gazes between one tree with a bear, many trees with no bears, and the two masters, as if watching some bizarre three-way tennis match.

Zane focused on the bruin up the tree at the end of his rope, while Bobby tried to calm the feisty hounds.

"Hey, shut it," said Bobby, in a deep tone to remind them who the master was. "You're scarin' the horse. And the cattle, too. Jesus. It's just a sweet baby black bear. You're supposed to hunt lions," said Bobby, reminding the mighty russet dinosaur-looking dog, a breed with an eponymous name of a place that no longer existed. "And you're just a dingo mutt," he said to the pigeon blue-grey cattle herder from down under; a brilliant, bastard of a dog.

"Bobby, they may have a point," Zane said, his tone filled with concern. "This one's momma or a friend might still be in there looking for him."

Bobby rolled his eyes and guffawed but hesitated as he considered the comment. "Right, true enough," said Bobby. "Fair point you got there, Zane. I'll grab the rifle, just in case."

Bobby left his horse by the corral fence and left Zane with the bear, walking back towards the gate. His truck was parked parallel to Zane's truck, on the far side of the corral entrance.

Zane tightened his grip, laughing about the situation.

Snarling, the black bear struggled to maintain its balance on the skinny branch. The dogs barked, circling the area. The horse continued neighing and kicking by the fence. The cattle kept up their lowing and bawling, with incessant mooing, horrified in the prison of their own manure, huddling together like a school of fish in a captive trout pond.

Bobby was halfway between his truck and the gate when the second bear, this one large and brown, came lumbering out of the woods.

Zane saw the bear step out of the forest fringe at the identical exit of the black bear now under his leash. "Bobby, get the gun, now!" Zane said, screaming.

Startled, Bobby turned around to see Zane yelling, the noisy chaos of the domestic farm animals, and the black bear in a freak-out of a panic attack in the pine tree. The black bear was staring at the bigger bear from above, hanging in the tree as if it were a wounded crow knowing it was out of spare flaps to take it higher up the tree or into the sky. The brown mammal was enormous—no doubt the same one that had chased it right out of the forest.

Each of the living creatures stood in complete dread. In an ironic unison of commotion, they were all allies now: the ranchers and their pets, protectors, and products, and a little black bear, all one and the same; they were lined up versus the gargantuan grizzly, growling and grumbling.

"Christ!" said Bobby, yelling like a metal-head. He went sprinting to the truck like an Olympic medalist, one wearing muddy boots and tight jeans held in place with a belt fastened with a giant sterling silver buckle.

The grizzly stopped, weighing which way to wander. The disturbance around the tree was concentrating its focus, the bear stepping towards the circus by the lone pine. The grizzly bear let out a massive roar, sauntering forward without fear. The ridgeback and heeler backed up to Zane's side, the heeler sweeping Zane's boots, its tail brushing away at them as quick as the wings of a hummingbird. Zane looked between the grizzly, heading his way, and Bobby, springing out of the pick-up truck with the gun now in hand. The horse had had enough, taking off into the empty pasture. The black bear moaned in the tree, as if it knew that certain death, for all, was present.

Zane could hear the sweet, delicate clicking sound in the background: the chambering of a round. Perhaps Zane was the only one who heard it, but every creature could hear the even sweeter, more deafening, next sound.

Bang!

The animals turned around to see Bobby, but the shooter was only looking for the grizzly's attention.

Bobby jogged towards the grizzly, getting in closer and at a better angle. He ejected the spent brass case, as a warning shot over the bear's head, and re-actioned the rifle. With the lever back in place, he lifted the stock and took minimal sight. The giant bruin stood up on its hind legs, which seemed as thick as Douglas fir trunks. It growled and roared, lifting its front paws to its head, as if wanting to box the roper-rancher moving towards it. The bear was now showing Bobby who was boss. Until...

Bobby fired again.

Bang!

Click: bang! Click: bang! Click: bang!

With four rounds of .30-06 in a tight pattern in its chest, the titanic *Ursus arctos horribilis* tottered, collapsing. With final forward momentum, the bear landed, sprawling out on its belly as though already a large tanned soft rug on the oak floor in front of a wood-burning fireplace. The bear was flailing as it was still able, twitching out its surely final movements, yet rolling over to its back, still up for some sort of a fight—a fight for its life this fight with Bobby, if no longer with the tiny black bear, almost a kid's stuffed animal by comparison.

The eyes of Bobby and Zane met as they were heading towards the grisly scene with the grizzly. Bobby did not seem concerned about re-loading. Zane left the rope behind with the black bear still up in the tree.

"Oh, crap," said Bobby, pointing to the grizzly's neck. "Look here. He's tagged. Trackin' device."

They paused, looking at each other again, and looking back to the still-living, growling and moaning, partially paralyzed, trying-to-fight bear.

"What's that mean, endangered?" Zane said, genuinely unsure. "But that's self-defense, right? It has to be."

"Well, probably, yeah," said Bobby, wanting to explain further yet becoming frantic. "But yeah, they're endangered. That's why they're trackin' them so closely."

For a silent few seconds, their thoughts were racing.

"I don't want a bunch of government types around here," said Bobby, with determination. "You know, lookin' around the farm. We've got some things here we shouldn't have, right? Plus, they might start thinkin' we're too close to the park...the ranch. All those officials, they don't know anything. They might cause us all sorts of other problems...farmin' and the other stuff. Man, we just don't want 'em here, bottom line. Look, we have to get rid of this thing, now."

"OK," Zane said, growing nervous. "I'll get more ammo from your truck. And I'll get the saw...we'll cut right through it."

"No, no time," said Bobby, as he ran off back to the truck himself.

Zane looked around, his tension escalating. He stood just far enough from and over the grizzly bear, ensuring he would not get hit by any last second wind the bear might conjure up. Zane was also worrying officials would already be on their way to the ranch. He noticed the black bear had made its way down the tree and was now running off into the pasture to the other side of where the horse went, ropes and reins drooping from the animals. The dogs had joined the cousins, now standing behind them, looking at the immense furry mocha torso thrashing about in the mud and blood.

"We have to do this now, and quick," said Bobby, on return to the scene.

Bobby was loading the gun (a different gun) one shell at a time, out of his pocket and into the port. Zane, perplexed at the change of firearm, watched on.

"I don't carry extra rounds for the rifle," said Bobby. "I've never needed more than were in the gun to take down any game around here. But in any event, always good to carry a shotgun with you. If I miss with the monster round, I sure's shit ain't missin' with buckshot."

Zane stood with greater ease, even if a level of uncertainty remained. He took out his Buck knife, dutifully preparing to do the dirty work of the jabbing and sawing of sinews, tendons, and bone, once the ultimate demise was unmistakable.

"OK, stand back," said Bobby, giving a stark warning.

"To end this, dear bear, here and now..."

Click: bang! Click: bang! Click: bang!

The rifle rounds in the chest were now dwarfed by the huge cavity of buckshot, having drilled the fur and lead-enveloped heart into the wet dirt beneath.

"And now, for the rug, minus head..."

Click: bang! Click: bang!

Bobby reached down, pulling one of the bear's ears to see how loose its mashed-up head and neck were, like that of a child and their miniature bear as plush teddy, hanging by a frayed thread no more. Bobby stood back up with the shotgun, moving in at an angle and almost point-blank range.

Click: bang! Click: bang! Click: bang!

This time, Bobby did not need to lift an ear, as the entire skull was pulverized—nothing remained above the collar but a mound of crimson jelly. With a kick at the top of the torso and a shove from the bottom of his boot, Bobby rolled the tracking collar from the bear's now non-existent head. Handing the gun to Zane, Bobby crouched down, grabbing the collar from the gory ground.

"Alright, we need to get this thing the hell out of here," said Bobby. "And fast."

Bobby looked around to consider, while Zane looked up to Bobby.

"Can't we just destroy it?" Zane said, wanting to offer his creative counsel. "Crush it and burn it?"

"No, we're too late for that," said Bobby. "They could see this on the map right now. And we're close enough to town, they could be on their way here already...to come and tranq the bear and drag him back into the mountains. But if they're not watchin' in real-time, this would be the last signal, right here in the pasture. Shoot, right at the corral even. They'd know for sure, or at least suspect...we can't have that."

They paused to each take a breath and gather their thoughts.

"I've got it," said Bobby in a revelatory tone. "We need to split up...the duties. If they've been watchin' the monitor, they're comin'. You stay back and take care of this mess. Shovel this muck and shit into a hole here. Get the Cat—bucket's already on it—and haul this goddamn thing into the yard. Dump it right into the pit, soak it with fuel, torch it. Once it's been ablaze for a minute, put on a bunch of that dead scrub to cover it up—burns cleaner and smells like a normal farmyard fire."

"OK, no problem...done," said Zane, exuding some confidence. "Where are you going?"

"I'll get the horse out there," said Bobby, as he could still see it in the pasture. "We'll head down to the valley with this collar. Give it a good half hour to burn and dump one good load of dirt over top the pit. We can mop up the mess later. Then you hitch the trailer up and meet me at The Grill. Back the trailer in behind the building where no one parks, and we'll meet you there...be there in an hour."

Bobby ran to his truck, drove to the pasture, and retrieved the horse.

Zane ran to his truck, drove to the yard, and got the Cat.

Zane headed back to the scene while Bobby headed down towards the river.

*

After nearly an hour of riding horseback through the river valley, Bobby made it to the edge of town, at the meeting place: just below the parking lot behind The Grill.

After an hour of digging, hauling, dumping, burning, burying, hitching, and driving, Zane made it to the edge of town, at said meeting place.

The parking lot and general area back behind The Grill was vacant. Zane signaled Bobby to make his way up the steep hill and into the trailer. Bobby jumped out to meet Zane, securing the trailer door with the horse inside.

"Jesus, we have to get rid of that thing," Zane said, panicking as he looked at Bobby who was holding the still bloodied and lead-stained collar. "I thought you were going to toss it in the river or something?"

Zane's agitation was growing. His head had been darting around in every direction as he was looking out of the truck windows on the drive in. The new reality of being in town caused him greater nervousness, being spooked at each sound in the parking lot, river pathway below, and echoes from the town proper.

"Christ, Zane," said Bobby. "They're not gonna be after us. You weren't on a car chase on the way in. And we're not gonna see some city SWAT team crash in here. Look, at some point—I'd bet days or even weeks from now—the collar will alert some nerdy official jerkin' off in a hut in the park somewhere. If he has any brains, he'll give up when they find it, knowin' it's gone...and it's a damn good joke if they have any sense of humour. But you know what? If it causes some fuss, well...I don't mind one darn bit. Serves them nosy pricks right, botherin' us and the ranch all the time. Now let's dump this thing and go eat."

Zane had no choice but to calm down, deferring to his

older, wiser, and more composed cousin. He watched as Bobby took a quick look around, as if he were just now about to commit a crime on the street, like a theft or dealing drugs or some such. Zane followed Bobby, walking towards the dumpster at the side of the restaurant. Bobby was trying to subtly conceal the collar as he moved at a slightly faster pace than he otherwise would have walked. He lifted the somewhat ajar dumpster lid with one hand, took another quick look around as if to monitor every angle, then he tossed the tracking device into the scarlet steel commercial-sized garbage bin of the proprietor.

"There we go," said Bobby, smiling as he dusted off his hands and began the walk out front. "One bear down, two beers up."

"Actually, if you think about it, the plushy one got away, so two down, two up," Zane said, beginning to relax with the incident finally appearing to be over. "I might need more than just a couple of beers though."

\*

The Grill was their favourite place: a great stereotypical country and western dive bar on the edge of town by the river, with live music on stage at night and dead meat on the menu always; beer and BBQ cow and pig, and no bears.

They sat at a table near the bar, slightly off to one side of the dank, windowless room. The waitress, knowing the two regulars, automatically brought them two bottles of Coors Light, asking them if they also wanted their regular lunch: pulled pork and beef brisket, plus set sides. Confirming the order, they sat for several minutes without speaking, watching baseball highlights on the TV behind the bar as they sipped their beer, each replaying the horror in their individual minds, right until the moment their jam-packed plates arrived.

"Well, now wasn't that a fun morning we had us?" Zane said, beaming and breaking the silence and the fast, starting in on his coleslaw. He was relieved the hectic, adrenaline-pumping ordeal was behind them.

"Heh, it sure was, I'll have to admit it," said Bobby, replying with a smile of his own as he started to dig into his dish of baked beans. "Assume your pet baby black bear there made it back to the woods, if not all the way back to the mountains. Unless he was so terrified he just kept on headin' east into the fields."

"Yeah, poor thing was going to be lunch for that big ole grizz," Zane said, chuckling. "Was it a male, or did you check?"

"Actually, never did. Meant to, but too busy takin' it apart...the grand decapitation. But must've been...colossal hulk like that, had to be."

"Yep, I wonder if those dogs weren't hungry," Zane said. "We could've left the guts for them. Yeesh. Now, if we had some pigs out there, well, that'd be another story...would've saved me some work."

\*

Almost done with their lunch, Bobby sopped up his chili with a side order bun, while Zane finished his dessert-like corn bread last.

"Well, let's settle up with her and get back there," said Bobby. "We can draw straws for who cleans up the pit."

"Forget that," Zane said. "I've had enough blood and

dirt and gas and smoke and all that business for today. But other than a bit of mud, there's not much to clean up, truth be told. Lemon squeezy, incineration easy-peasy."

"Heh, you said it," said Bobby, flagging down the waitress for their bill.

They sat for another few minutes, giving further time for reflection, waiting patiently for the tab. The waitress returned, without a bill in hand—instead, she delivered two more Silver Bullets to the table.

"I've got some good news and some bad news for you boys," she said, winking and smiling. "Bad news is: you can't leave right now. Cops just showed up out there...couple of cars, lights flashing. They almost tackled the busboy when he was taking out the trash. Said there's a vicious bear out there, and no one can go anywhere till the area's all clear. Must have come into town up the river valley, they say. Anyways, the good news is: another beer for you fine fellas."

A stunned look overtook Zane. Bobby smiled. Again, they sipped their bottles in silence until they were almost empty, trying to take their minds off the immediate search right outside the tacky cedar-paneled walls. They were continuing to focus on the TV screen behind the bar...

\*

The front door creaked as George and Corb walked into the bar. They looked relaxed, even if in their official work clothes, while also appearing to be in need of a beer and a late lunch.

"Well, look at that: the roping star," said George, the local conservation officer. "And his good cousin. How you boys doing today?"

"Don't mind if we join you for a beer now, do you?" said Corb, the town sheriff.

"Well, not at all," said Bobby, with a calm, pleasant smile. "Just about to order another round, in fact. Waitress said we can't leave the bar with you guys huntin' bears out there."

Zane's stress returned, but he was managing a slight grin and awkward giggle as the waitress brought the round of four cold bottles to the table.

"Oh, we got us our bear," said George. "He ate his way through some leftovers out back. Ate so much he totally decomposed himself...not even a shred of enamel left from those huge ole canine teeth. Only his radio collar remains. Incredible stuff. Almost like sci-fi, this case."

"Well, bears don't do too well around this here chili," said Bobby, with a natural chuckle. "Peppers are so spicy in there, the gas burns right through the back of your Wranglers. Can't imagine how enamel would weather it."

"Ha!" said Corb, laughing aloud, lacking the authenticity of Bobby's. "You know, he'd been in your boys' area this mornin'. Parks crew asked if we'd mind checkin' the area...those lazy rats. We went out there, but you boys weren't around. And what the hell you guys doin' with all that dirt you're pushin' around in the yard? Good lord, what a mess. Can't imagine what it looks like in the barn and house. Anyways, that bear sure made it to town quick, don't you think?"

"Now, gents, what my good colleague here is trying to say is," said George, between sips. "We don't like playing hide and seek, and we hate all them chase games...it's like grab-ass, but without the real fun, the score. You want a good clean, safe game to play? I'll tell you: shoot, shovel, and shut up! You just need to think through each step when you play it, so you don't miss anything...it's a real strategic game. And you have to have the right tactics, too. If you want to win the game, that is. But bottom line is: you want to play those other games, then go the other way...go do it in the mountains. Parks guys love those silly games. But we don't like them here in town."

"That's right," Corb said, backing up his colleague while trying to remain relevant in the conversation. "Best keep a close watch on your livestock goin' forward. Keep your eyes open, dogs hungry, and guns loaded. And keep them games on the ranch or go west. George and I agree: no goddamn games in town."

All four sat for a few seconds in silence, then took an unplanned but synchronized sip of their beers.

"But enough about bears and chases and shit," said George. "We're all nice and safe now, with that poor vaporized grizzly bear. So cheers to that."

Bobby and Zane were getting a rough ride of fear and guilt and confusion yet trying to follow the lead of George and Corb. The four bottles clanked together over the middle of the table in a more jovial air and with a requisite verbal chorus of 'cheers.'

"Now, on to more important matters," said George. "Bobby, tell us about that great win you just had that we all heard about, last weekend down the road. And what's your plan for our modest rodeo here this weekend? Everyone in town is going to be there, rooting you on."

# Saint Lazarus Day

I wasn't sure if I was in a hospital, holding cell, the afterlife, or some strange dream-state. I couldn't tell if I was recounting the incidents to doctors and nurses, guards and agents, deities and devils, or just to myself. But I remembered certain events...

The first thing I recall was that my goal was to cross the two borders and flout U.S. Customs on the return trip. I drove straight to the airport in Montréal from my college town in New England, heading west at first then taking Interstate 87 north in upstate New York, having no issues at that crossing—not even a line-up. Succeeding through the labyrinth of decrepit Québec roads, I got to the airport, took off, landed, and asked these new customs agents, who were dressed from head-to-toe in a drab olive green instead of the dark navy-blue uniform of home:

"*Por favor, no estampe mi pasaporte.*"

"Hmm, *tu no eres americano,*" the agent said, frowning then smiling as he was reviewing my passport, as he knew. "*Ah, pero sí. No hay problema.* Enjoy."

"*¡Gracias!*" I said, relieved. "*Muchas gracias, señor.*"

A college friend from Florida had arranged for me to stay the first week with some of his non-immediate family. He said I would have fun with the locals while acclimatizing myself to the climate and the culture. It was a midsize town on the coast about two hours from the airport, away from the city and off the beaten path. One of his cousins, Luis, picked me up at the stifling airport.

His car of a fading aquamarine was an odd beast, built up from seemingly sundry random parts—it looked like an ancient 1950s Packard and some 1970s Soviet piece of shit, all fused together somehow, as if a form of junky contemporary art, but having a real and practical purpose, with the semi-functional engine and wheels. Luis drove me and my unstamped passport to the home of him and his wife, Claudia. The car stalled in the city and smoked on the highway—the charcoal plumes of the diesel fumes had a dizzying effect, exacerbating my nausea from the turbulent landing. But we eventually made it to their town...

The family welcomed me with a great feast already set out on my arrival, as if I was some notable dignitary or an exotic guest. It seemed as if the whole neighbourhood was there for the dinner of salad, rice and beans, pan-fried white fish, something I wasn't sure if it was chicken or pork or beef—the meat smelled alright if not great, yet it tasted good enough. I noticed what I thought was cut up papaya in long, fresh slices on one plate—the dinner party had a good laugh when I named the fruit, unaware as I was of the local jargon concerning *la fruta bomba*. We also had milkshakes made of mamey, which I had to look up as well. Bottles of *el ron* were passed around as if they were tap water, so we drank lots of that island hooch. The meal was excellent—I had a serious hunger from the flight and drive. But I drank too much in the course of the evening, this exciting start to my back-packing adventure.

"*¡Muchas gracias!*" I said. I said this over and over all evening, like a broken record, *ad* freaking *nauseum*.

I had a good sleep that first night and my host brought me eggs, more papaya and other fruit, and some leftovers in the morning. Then I walked over to the beach in the early heat. Their house was near the sea. The sea wall was half a block away—the nice part of *la playa* was only another block down.

The port town was set at the centre of a large bay. The horseshoe shape seemed to go on forever before reaching the ocean on either side. There was some activity on the far side of the bay from me, in what looked like an archaic industrial harbour that was abandoned long ago. I spent most of the day getting some sun, reading, taking a dip in the sea, watching the locals mill about: they were walking, beachcombing, swimming, playing, fishing, boating, and sitting around not doing too much of anything, often with mangy dogs hanging about—I saw a fair number of those sad creatures.

I often looked back towards the town proper, watching the patched up rickety cars driving by in front of the dilapidated pastel façades of time-worn buildings on the road, just behind the exposed and also derelict *malecón*, the concrete crumbling away.

A middle-aged man strolled along the sidewalk behind me pushing an ice cream cart. Catching my eye, he explained what he had for sale. I had no problem accepting the offer of *el helado de mango*, paying him well for it. I ate it as quick as I was able before it melted, dripping away in the intense heat and humidity. He tried to sell me more ice cream, but I wanted to get back to the sun and my book. I told the vendor with the ice cream cart what I'd really like was a cold beer or two.

"*¿Cerveza?*" I said, motioning a sip from a phantom bottle.

"*¿Una cerveza?* Beer?" he said. The vendor had a serious tone and look about him as he was considering my question, as if I was challenging him to produce some rare and mystical item, this chilly can of rotten barley.

"*Sí, sí,*" said the ice cream man, suggesting perhaps it was possible to obtain such a difficult to find product. "*Usted deme unos minutos.* Um, *minutos*—few minutes." He darted off with his cart back towards the town centre...

He returned about ten minutes later with a cool can in each hand: a Cristal and a Mayabe. "*Las cervezas.* Beer!" he said, smiling as if triumphant. We bartered for a moment, but of course I was wanting the beers I'd asked for, so I bought both cans—rejecting beers I'd ordered was the absolute last thing I'd do at that point. It turned out he was now charging me in the local currency, different than the original ice cream currency, although for that I had waved a green bill out before we had a chance to properly negotiate on the mango cone. He tried to give me change, but when I did the quick math in my head, I realized I was paying only a few mere cents per can of beer. I rejected the change, giving him way more than the original asking spot price. I asked him to come back in *una hora con dos cervezas más.* Then one more time after that. I think ice cream sales had ceased for the day, as the vendor was busy sourcing his new product line and figuring out all the complex supply chain logistics, with me on the beach as his sole distribution center or retail outlet. I hadn't been there twenty-four hours and I felt like I already had my own personal beer monopoly, or at least beer butler.

After several hours in the sun (and an ice cream, six beers, and no lunch nor water), I was bagged and starting to feel it. And I was getting these itchy little red marks on my skin, seemingly all over my legs—they were mild if noticeable when I woke up, becoming worse each hour that passed by. I wasn't sure if it was maybe the gritty sand, impure water, glaring sun, some food allergy or reaction—maybe a combination of several of those various effects. Still, I decided to walk around and explore the area a bit more before dinner.

I headed up the hill off the bay towards the old cathedral, which sat above the town. I looked around the abandoned church and ruins, and down to the bay and town from the stunning birds-eye view. Then I hiked down the opposite side of the hill to the neglected sugarcane fields. They were now in a dense, near-jungle state. I wandered along the abandoned railway right-of-way. My guidebook cited a steam train owned by the Hershey chocolate interest had hauled cane out of the fields to make sugar at one time, but no more. I couldn't imagine chocolate bars back home originating here, as it looked like the farming operation was let go many decades ago, kind of a tropical version of parts of the contemporary Rust Belt, or a rural adaptation of parts of modern Detroit, or so I thought.

I ended up back at the bay, but on the other side of it, not far from the rusty tanker port. I was thirsty, hungry, exhausted—I was dehydrated and had some sunstroke or maybe heat exhaustion, perhaps a bit of both. The marks on my skin were still itchy, becoming a darker reddish colour like a scarlet, and they were almost sore with a kind of bumpiness to them. They were starting to drive me mad, even more so realizing I didn't bring any calamine lotion along on the trip, although I wasn't sure that it would have done much to help my current state.

I walked the entire length of the *malecón* path back to my spot on the beach, then over to the house. I'd swatted a few mosquitos on the walk around the cathedral ruins and former cane fields, and I was now noticing I had a few bites from my post-beach trek. I wondered if the bad fevers still existed here: yellow, dengue, malaria, whatever else. The Hershey chocolate mosquitos longed for the hundreds of cane workers, but only got my lonely gringo tourist blood today.

To take my mind off of the bites, I started to sing to myself: "Mosquito sing, mosquito cry, mosquito live, mosquito die, mosquito drink, most anything, whatever's left, mosquito scream, I'll suck your blood..." But that just reinforced my problem, the severe itching and illing on my legs and elsewhere.

When I made it back to the house, Claudia was in the front yard, her mocha skin radiating around her frayed sleeveless shirt and tight jean shorts. She was chatting with the neighbour as they stood by the red and white poinsettias in full bloom near the gate. *Christmas in the Caribbean!* I thought. They asked me about my day and invited me to a party that evening—Vicente, the neighbour she was talking to, was hosting it. I was excited about the function, which they tried to describe to me, in part broken English and part Spanish, saying it was an important annual cultural event in town, but basically it was just a good, fun time. I said I'd love to go, obviously. I went inside to clean up, hydrate, and eat something.

I had a quick bite of the leftover meat, some new rice and beans, and colourful fresh fruit. I sat with my host family, who were also going across the street to join the festivities. After dinner, I went to my room to check out my guidebooks, as I wanted to know what the party was all about. With the history and mystery, it sounded like great fun. One book said:

> *Santería,* or saint worship, has been deeply entrenched in Cuban culture for 300 years. The cult is a fusion of Catholicism with the Lucumi religion of the African Yoruba tribes...since slave masters had banned African religious practice, the slaves cloaked their gods in Catholic garb and continued to pray to them...Catholic figures are avatars of the Yoruban *orishas* (divine beings of African animism worshipped in secret and complex rituals...The gods are believed to perform all kinds of miracles on a person's behalf...Almost every home has a statue of a santería god...*Santería* is a sensuous religion. It lacks the arbitrary moral prescriptions of Catholicism—the *orishas* let adherents have a good time.

Sure enough, I read further on in my other guidebook that one important *Santería* holiday in December is Saint Lazarus Day. Worshipping healing miracles, praying for health, blah, blah, blah... The other book had me at "have a good time."

"Outstanding," I said, aloud and to myself. "My first full day here and already a goddamn *Santería* party! ¡*Viva Cuba!*

"I don't practice *Santería*, I ain't got no crystal ball, well I had a million dollars but I, I'd spend it all," I sang to myself, thrilled about the imminent event.

I imagined rum, cigars, girls. That would be so great. Or really two of any of the three would work out just fine, if I was being true and honest with myself.

I was still a bit buzzed from the beer, a bit heat-stroked and/or -exhausted from the sun, and I started wondering if my first few meals were causing some gastro issues— something felt as if it wasn't settling or digesting properly. I drank two glasses of tap water, which I quickly realized was no doubt an idiot rookie traveler mistake in a place like this—a hint of something to make it that much worse, and that I'd then start puking and shitting myself any second, hopefully not in front of the local ladies. However, I felt I needed the fluid to hydrate myself. I longed for a keg-sized bottle of lemon-lime Gatorade—what I would have done for one of those, or even the gross orange-flavoured kind would have done just fine. I put a basic lotion on my worsening bites and bumps, covering them up with jeans, then joining Luis and Claudia, walking across the street to Vicente's party.

We walked straight into his living room through a thick fog of cigar smoke. The authenticity of the aroma smelled fantastic. A man near the door offered me a cigar out of a box sitting on a bookshelf he stood next to—I was used to the exact opposite, with a bouncer collecting the cover charge from me back home, not giving me a gift on arrival. I was happy to oblige the present from this man who looked like he was straight out of the Buena Vista Social Club.

"*¡Gracias!*" I said, smiling at the man. The cigar was long like a Churchill and thick like a *Robusto*: it was an enormous tight roll of who knows how many tobacco leaves weaved together by hand. I could only see the classic *Habanos* sticker and stamp on the box, so I wasn't sure of the exact brand, but they all seemed quite similar to my amateur non-cigar aficionado palate. I was handed a lighter—I struggled to light it and keep it lit. When I did succeed, the smell and taste of the cigar was great. But the smoke hit me fast: my smoke, the smoke of others, the systemic smoke cloud lingering throughout the house. It was like a tobacco-based tear gas bomb went off in his tiny, square concrete home.

Claudia was chatting with a couple of her friends, while the party host, Vicente, escorted me through the thick smoke and crowd of people into the equally packed kitchen. Several bottles of rum sat on a small kitchen table. None of the bottles had labels, and *el ron* was clear—the liquid wasn't crystal clear and it wasn't filtered, but at the same time it wasn't the thick dark molasses-like demerara rum known from around the region and the days of old, the grog of pirates. The guests were drinking it straight out of small glasses. They kept pouring more for each other—another gent handed me one of the glasses and poured.

The rum was potent, having some extreme level of proof. The smoke in the room, the cigar in my mouth, and the rum in various stages of flowing throughout my body hit me hard and fast. Combined with the earlier food, beer, and sun (and maybe mosquitos), my light buzz turned to a heavy dizzy, in a hurry. I knew I needed to control myself, but that's when the party got going. That's when Vicente brought me back into the living room with the others, as he wanted to begin the formal ceremonial proceedings, whatever those were going to be.

The room quieted down. The guests continued smoking and drinking, in silence and with some degree of anticipation. We stood in front of the living room mantle with our eyes focused towards it. Vicente grabbed my hand and the hand of the other guy closest to him, then the group held hands at odd angles, forming a kind of spiderweb. Then each person closed their eyes as if beginning a group meditation or preparing for some sort of trance. Vicente started talking, slow and quiet at first, then quicker and louder, again and again—it was like a Nirvana song, without the guitars and drums. The partygoers rocked and jittered at their own pace and motion, each in their own independent and concurrent euphoria, respectively. Some swayed back and forth, together in unison and on their own, now grasping hands but with their eyes closed, becoming anarchic. It was turning into a bizarre frenzy, as if we were like Baptists of the West Indies or something, in a collective hallucination, bobbing about.

After a minute or so of this odd prelude, Vicente offered a prayer to the ornamental Jesus-like statue on the mantle. A note of thankfulness became a fury of yelling and babbling, singing to and at the statue. The group continued rocking back and forth while facing the voodoo-esque figurine surrounded by a variety of burning candles. The people were dancing and humming to themselves, yet on some level they were trying to follow the ritualistic rhythm of their good leader, Vicente. With no apparent structure, it became incoherent—at least to me it did.

Vicente took a swig of rum directly from a bottle, showing the burn in his eyes as he shuddered and cranked his neck after downing it—his drunken hum and gurgle with a scrunched-up face showing everyone his discomfort with the swallow. He took another sip, hesitating and keeping it, feeling it in his mouth this time, swishing it a bit like mouthwash. Pursing his lips, he leaned back and then leapt forward, letting the rum go in a spray of fine alcoholic mist out of his sprinkler-like mouth and onto the statue, a wet sugary shrapnel stoking the ceremonial candles, hitting everyone and everything around him.

The party host continued his prayer, asking the idol to bring good health to family and friends. He even said a few things in English for me, praying for me and my family, our health and welfare, my safe travels, that sort of thing. While my guidebooks proved accurate, I also thought this was a great irony, as the effects from the sun, beer, food, water, mosquitos, and whatever else from my first day here, and now the booze and plumes of cigar haze, were intensifying the dizzying effect. I was in a near hallucinatory spin at this point, messed right up.

Yeah, I was pretty drunk when the *ceremonia de Santería* ended and the party just sort of went back to a normal pace: more rum in the kitchen, more cigars in the living room. I had to get outside and get some fresh air to clear my head, plus I thought I might puke so better to do that out of the house—there had been enough spewing in that home, and I didn't want to ralph on the voodoo Jesus,

45

at least not without the essential and pure rum.

I stumbled across the street and leaned against the sea wall, managing to vomit over it. The open air of the ocean breeze and accompanying mist felt great on my face, and on the back of my neck and head as I turned around—it was a similar consistency to the rum spray, but cool and fresh, and without more smoke. I wiped my mouth of vomit remnants with one hand and wiped my face of mist with the other, then let more mist on: a cleansing and refreshing feeling (even if a bit salty), alleviating the sick feeling, somewhat...

I went back into the smoke where a stunning *señora* poured me a rum, gripping a clean glass in my hand, with her one hand on mine. I hadn't seen her in the house earlier, this flawless dream girl goddess with her striking cocoa complexion—I couldn't reject anything she offered. She rubbed against me in the overcrowded room, then turned to take the bottle back into the kitchen, leaving me with an exotic and glamorous smile.

*Saint Lazarus to the rescue*, I thought, in my besotted state. *The sea, and she, woke me.* Or so I believed, I wished.

I looked down to Vicente, who sat on a chair under the mantle. He looked like he was about to pass out, his head bobbing around with heavy eyes, a cigar hanging out of his lips with an equal length of leaf and ashes dangling from his mouth.

Then I had another errant wave of nausea. Attempting to go back to the *malecón*, I puked again before reaching it and then just stumbled home. I remember that, and that my body was quite sore, like I had the full-on flu with all the accompanying symptoms imaginable, and then some. Other sequences in time and of events I can't recall as well:

in the voodoo party house, outside, deciding to then head to bed—some things I just don't remember on how the evening played out, fumbling about in my daze towards the end of the event.

I woke up in my room in the morning, still sore and a bit drunk, but on my way to the critical hangover phase. The ceiling continued spinning with what seemed to be more of an almost psychoactive quality than solely of drunkenness. I figured this was the strong rum and cigar effect, plus all the other stuff from the day before, so I slept in and out for a few more hours.

It was about noon when Claudia came in with a late breakfast. That's when I realized I couldn't move. My muscles ached; I felt paralyzed. Yet, incredibly, my drunkenness and hangover were gone. She didn't understand, and neither did I. I was terrified, to the point where after a few minutes I shook and teared up—I didn't know what the hell was happening. I couldn't move at all, laying there completely motionless. I couldn't properly communicate with her, but she ran out of the room and came back in minutes with Luis first, then Vicente, and then a doctor named Roberto. All the while, I had been contemplating: what the hell was this about?

The food: fresh and E. coli leftovers, sundry mystery street meats of botulism, unpasteurized mango ice cream or mamey milkshake of listeriosis?

The sun: burn, stroke, heat exhaustion, haze?

The drink: beers at the beach, tap water, who knows what percentage of alcohol and production method of the party rum, a roofie within?

The smoke: mammoth cigars, second-hand concussive clouds, a bit of synthetic something else wrapped up in the leaf?

The voodoo: prayers to the patron saint of health, *Santería* spell on the unsuspecting foreigner, exotic touch or curse of the local goddess?

I was so scared. How did this happen and what was next? Was I going to die in this dumpy rural hole of a tropical town, where I wasn't supposed to be and no one back home even knew where I was (save for my college friend, who in turn was not known by anyone in my family either)? *Oh, my good freaking lord—I'm going to die here,* I thought. It was all I could think as my head was racing.

The doc looked unconcerned or indifferent at first, soon growing at least a bit flummoxed—he was thinking now, trying to diagnose my mysterious condition. Claudia spoke quickly, explaining the events since my arrival: drive, meals, beach, hike, party, etc. Then a hungover Vicente described the party: cigars, rum, prayers for health, etc. I caught a few words from the discussion (*ron, cigarro, sol*) and as much or more from their mannerisms (tone of voice, eye movement, arms and hands waving about).

The room went silent as those present considered the situation. Vicente stepped on a bug with his weathered tan sandals. The crowd adjusted their positions and kept pondering the circumstances. Vicente looked down to another bug, reached out of his way with his leg this time, squashing the second one, as he then closed his eyes and grabbed his aching hungover head. He noticed a third insect climb up the wall behind the headboard of my bed, making a joke to Claudia about the bugs and her poor hosting or house cleaning, or some such.

Claudia looked embarrassed but laughed it off. Dr.

Roberto looked to me and towards his medical bag, then let out a concentrated "hmm" as he thought further. With two insects squished on the floor, and third and fourth bugs now climbing the wall behind my head, the good doc looked like he had an epiphany, saying he wanted to check something out. He lifted and pulled the sheet from my legs, then rolled my left pant leg up. I could tell by his reaction, followed by the same look of Vicente, Claudia, and Luis, that it wasn't good news; no, it was terrible news.

"Could bed bugs do this," I asked myself. I couldn't feel anything too itchy or painful on my skin any longer, but my muscles weren't working, and my stomach now had sharp pains throbbing in and out every minute or so, as if I was passing kidney stones or having contractions, if not a knife twisting in my torso, or so I imagined. Roberto removed the sheet entirely. I saw the bumpy red marks all over my right forearm, looking thick and swollen. A few looked like they were festering, with bits of blood and puss seeping out. It was as gross as it gets.

Vicente flicked another bug off the wall and stepped on another, then jumped back from the bed. The doc got down on his knees, giving himself a bit of distance to look under the bed, moving closer in a calculated manner to get a better view of the culprit bugs.

"Oh, *Jesucristo*," Doctor Roberto said, in a concerned tone, as if he wasn't a doctor. But he was a physician, as they had already assured me earlier.

"*Las arañas*. Eh, uh, a spider. Spiders," he said, moving his fingers through the air as if his hand was a spider out for a walk, a new interpretation of the ascending Itsy Bitsy Spider. "*El nido*. Ah, a nest. Big nest. Many spiders."

Roberto motioned for the other three to stand back. Then things got going for real.

"*Usted llame a la ambulancia,*" the doctor said to Claudia.

Then he said a few other things to her, where I could hear within the sentences: *hospital, intravenoso, tóxico,* and *Habana.*

The doctor signaled for Luis and Vicente to help him lift me off the bed and out of the room.

"*Hospital,*" he said, enunciating the words to me slowly, one syllable at a time. "You need *hospital.*"

For emphasis, Roberto drew the universal and capital 'H' with his fingers as he said hospital, which seemed unnecessary, as the word was the same in either language, albeit minus the silent 'h' here.

They carried me outside, setting me down on the untidy grass next to the blooming poinsettias by the gate in the front yard. It wasn't the fish or pork or whatever I ate. It wasn't the sun or beers. It wasn't the cigars or rum. I hadn't ruled out a magic spell...*Santería.* But no, it was just a few little bug bites in my room. And spiders, not bed bugs nor chocolate-loving mosquitos. Either way, it was nothing but some wretched insects.

"*El nido of las arañas,*" I said, as if now was a good time to practice my Spanish.

"You be OK, but hospital," Roberto said again, trying to reassure me.

"*Los relojes de arena.* Um, the *hora...*" he said, considering this translation as he looked to Luis and Vicente to see if they knew the English word.

"*Sí,*" said Vicente. He used his finger like the doctor to draw through the air in front of me. I thought he was referring to a clock or time, as he drew the dizzying motion of an '8', twice to be sure. Then he tipped the '8' in an upside-down motion with his hand and said, "*Hora.* Hourglass. *Rojo.*"

Claudia had returned. She, Luis, Vicente, and Roberto looked at one another and down at me. They looked at me like I was mortally wounded, if not already a messed-up maggoty corpse polluting their verdant yard with my decomposition.

Luis closed his eyes, shook his head, crossed himself, and said something in his prayer about *Jesús* and *San Lázaro*. Then he did the same thing to me.

That was it. That was the point when I understood what had happened, or at least that part of the incident. My own revelation: the red hourglass. I'd only just studied this in biology last semester. I still didn't understand the gravity of it, but I wasn't sure if that even mattered at this stage. *Fuck me*, I thought. Crude and banal as it was, it was all I could think.

Two of the neighbourhood feral dogs came running over to where I was lying on the grass. They were trying to lick my arms and legs. Doctor Roberto and Luis worked to shoo them away, flailing away while yelling at them.

I leaned my head back with the minimal movement I had in my neck, and I looked straight up at a coconut palm. A stereotypical warm tropical breeze moved in and shook the fronds above me, themselves below the cerulean sky much further above. My muscles were beyond sore, the pain in my stomach ached as if I was about to pass stones or give birth, and I was losing my sentience in this scene of an otherwise Cuban cliché. I wished a giant coconut would fall from the tree and strike me dead; an unimpeded heavyweight-like blow from the husk and shell of that one ripe fruit would surely do it from that height.

The ambulance arrived. It was a van that had seen better days. I was barely conscious, I was in serious pain, I still couldn't move. Claudia handed my wallet and passport to Vicente, who thumbed through it with Roberto. The doctor spoke to the paramedics. The best I could make out was he said something like:

"Here is the sick man. His name is John. He is lying here by our gates, covered in bites. He is from the town of Bethany, in *Norteamérica*. He is going to sleep but we are trying to keep him awake. We are comforting him."

This sounded so familiar, like from a story—almost of a biblical verse or something. But in my state, I couldn't place it, or anything else at that point or thereafter.

As the paramedics and Roberto lifted me into the old ambulance, I looked to Vicente and thought about his rum-spraying prayer to the figurine.

That was the last thing I recall: Saint Lazarus. And fresh papaya. I don't remember anything else after that.

# The Engineer

"What's it like, him standing there, compared to a nothing deer or something you see all the time out there?" said the cop, sipping his coffee while sitting across the aged square steel interrogation table from the engineer. "I assume you've seen quite a lot on the line, across the west."

"I sure have, alright. A lot more than I'd have liked to have seen, in fact," said the old engineer, leaning back in his hard chair, speaking slowly. "Deer, mostly. They're a dime a dozen, no matter where you are these days— they've got ample food anywhere they look nowadays, and fewer predators, hunters. You don't hear them or feel them, don't care if you see them or not. Immense ones are different though. Watching an elk or moose explode in front of you is...it's something else. Hitting a bull moose...Christ, it's like running into a cinderblock wall of guts and gore. A mess of blood and fur and shit all over the front."

"You mean you see that in the daytime?" said the cop, imagining the grotesque visual as seen through the engineer's eyes. "I thought it was only at night they jumped out like that."

"Well, partly," said the engineer. "Some are so dumb they just stand there in the day. Lots have the CJD disease now, turns them into zombie cervids. But dusk and dawn, more often. And night, for sure. You don't see it all, but you see enough and you know. Deer and whatnot, you see their eyes, way down the line. Their eyes glow, like moon dogs radiating off them, creating a halo around their heads. They have a laser-like focus, totally stunned or hypnotized by the light coming at them. It's a piercing porcelain white stare, as if they're already a ghost and they know it. Back when I was a conductor, a veteran colleague I worked with would yell out the window, *Stay away from the light,* like they'd understand that. No, not those stupid things."

The cop and the engineer looked at one another, each considering the incredulous mindset of these creatures, the deer of such pitiful and foreign brains.

The engineer continued his explanation:

"With deer, the closer you get, its head might jerk one way or another, then up or down, like a boxer moving to avoid the jab or lead and trying to figure out the counterpunch. But there's no counter coming from these idiots. Anyways, they do that dizzying butterfly dance, as if preparing to spar, but all they're doing is getting ready for the smack-down, that heavy KO punch, knocking them into another world. I saw a buck once, standing on the right side, leaning in a bit as he bobbed to and fro. His head was perfectly sheared off. The antlers hit the windshield, cracked the glass, a shower of blood, torso pulverized into stewing meat."

"Jesus, and I thought I saw all nasty stuff," said the cop,

chuckling. "You'd never see the varmints, I imagine...too puny. What about bears?"

"Yep, lots of bears around these days, especially during harvest, close to the mountains or tree line, on the fringe of the forest belt," said the engineer. "Black bears, that is. They eat berries and whatever along the right-of-way, like fields of oats, which they love. But they'll usually get out of the way. If the big momma has cubs near, she'll do her protective thing. I hit one like that once. Cocky bitch, standing up to a machine like that. Futile, sweetheart."

"So true," said the cop, using his fingers to play with his moustache as he considered this incident. "Hmm..."

"You don't see grizzlies often, and usually only up in the mountains," said the engineer. "I only ever hit one once, and in daytime, of all things. He was standing next to a fresh elk carcass just off the rail, on the aggregate. The elk must have got hit by the train right before mine. The grizzly looked aged and confused, probably blind or something. He was sniffing the air trying to locate the animal...they don't normally eat dead things, so that made it even more confusing. But the bear kept on smelling, wandering around, trying to find a meal in his hungry confusion, right up to getting smoked. Poor bear's last breath would've been diesel and iron, not the tasty meat it was longing for."

"Yeah, the bear would've heard, smelled, and felt that, if it couldn't see it," said the cop. "You're supposed to have stronger other senses when you're down one, but not enough to realize death was right before it in that case. You ever see wolves and cougars on your mountain runs?"

"Yes, large cats and dogs," said the engineer. "It's a rare occurrence, because they're smart—they jump clear out of the way. Well, I guess I've hit feral mutts on sidings in towns, but not in the bush. I've seen those enormous brutes way down the line. But dog or cat, he'll be long gone before you get there. Heh, you know, I say 'he' or 'his,' as if I know the sexes. I don't, of course—minus an obvious momma with her cubs. I just know the outcome. It's always the same."

"No doubt—true, true, true," said the cop, slowing down his own words. "What about the female? Have you ever seen a girl there? I mean, a woman—a human woman?"

"Only once," said the engineer, in sharp tone of confirmation. "With animals, you don't know, normally. But you sure do know when it's people—a person. It's always a 'he.' You can be certain he's a male. You know better than me though...that's your business, not mine. Girls don't do that, right?"

"I've not seen one do it that way," said the cop, reminiscing briefly as if to confirm his own thoughts. "No, I don't believe I have."

"They take pills, cut themselves. Men shoot, blowing their brains out all over the basement. I guess both hang, and jump, sometimes," said the engineer, as if he did, in fact, now understand the policeman's business. "It's a bit funny, or odd at least, no one ever mentions a train. A train isn't thought of as an option, not around here. But let me tell you: it is an option. The train is as good an option as any of them others. Train accidents are more common than most would think."

"Well, it's a certain method, unlike the 'cry-for-help' types," said the cop, using finger quotations as if to better make the point. "Anything is certain if you do it right, but you won't have many failed attempts—the train offers that final dimension to it. Or I guess I should say, it *did* offer an absolute end."

"The only woman I ever saw was years ago, way before you would've been policing in the area, or policing at all," said the engineer, to the middle-aged and much younger cop. "It seemed like a suicide at first, but a while after they thought it might have been a homicide. She laid across the track, perpendicular, with her neck resting on one rail and legs on the other—only time I've seen it like that. I understand she had a history, bit of a transient, maybe whoring around and drugs and whatever, so could've been put there, or could've put herself there, I guess. We'll never know."

"Yikes, brutal," said the cop. "Poor thing. And a cold case forever, most likely, you're right."

They looked to the middle of the table from their seats, thinking about the girl, laid out like that, awaiting her permanent dismembered sleep. The cop played with his nickel tie clip attached to his cheap ugly maroon tie, rubbing the gaudy rayon accessory with his thumb, twisting the angle of it. The engineer played with his coffee mug, grasping the handle and rotating its position on the table, creating a gentle scratching sound on the rough metallic surface of the tabletop.

"And what about him?" asked the cop. "One of many, I take it? Many men, I mean. More boys than girls?"

"Yeah," said the engineer. "That poor bastard was the ninth one I've seen. Who knows how many I've missed seeing, but I know I've seen nine. The running score is eight to one. More antlers and horns, and many more varmints, but man, not woman...gents sit atop the totem pole on the line list. It's a sad thing, no two ways about it. Terribly sad."

"Hmm," said the cop, deep in thought. "And that was the first time you've shot someone like that? But I assume you've done the same to animals out there?"

"Oh, yes, certainly," said the engineer, smiling. "I've sprayed my share of deer, moose, elk—all those big game types. Not varmints though: too small, quick. Inconsequential. Almost impossible to hit at that speed, when you're just hanging out the door or have the window rolled down. And that's not a great gun. Christ, it's not much of a firearm at all, really...your aim is so poor. With a hulking, staring, hypnotized dummy standing there, it's much easier...you just keep firing as rapidly as you can and you're bound to hit him with at least a few rounds."

"Oh, man," said the cop, laughing. "You're a crazy son of a bitch, you are. Did you shoot that poor old blind bear?"

"No," said the engineer, grinning again. "That was before I decided to take the fun gun with me into the engine. No, haven't shot any bears, yet...but I will if I ever get the chance again, mark my words."

"Ok, ok," said the cop. "What in the Sam Hill a notion. I mean, where the hell do you come up with an idea like that? No one in here can even believe such a thing."

"Heh," said the engineer, chuckling. "Well, to tell you the truth, my grandson gave me the idea—creative wee rascal he is. He came for a ride one day, on a short line return trip—a quick run on a spur to get a few carloads of coal. There was a deer eating quackgrass growing out of the ties right on the branch line there...I guess he didn't like eating it from the slag piles nearby. We ran him over real good, right in the mid-morning, a beautiful blue sky kind of day. My grandson wasn't really bothered by it, thinking the whole circumstance was sort of annoying, for all parties."

"Heh," said the cop, laughing a bit harder. "Quite annoying for the deer, getting crushed and mutilated. A significant nuisance, I bet."

"Exactly," said the engineer. "Anyways, it was a pretty hot and humid day, so on the return trip, there's the rotting carcass, already festering in the rocks. He's covered in crows and vultures. Literally, those scavengers were sitting and dining there together, as if they were at a family reunion or a holiday meal, taking turns at this decomposing buffet. They'd still be bickering over carrion leftovers the next day, no question."

"Christ, that's sick," said the cop. "We're getting close to lunch now, so if you could leave out the grotesques and tell me about your grandson and his idea, the young marksman."

"Right, sorry," said the engineer. "Well, he just came up with the idea. He said he learned in his class how the pioneers used to shoot at herds of buffalo from the trains. I laughed, but then I thought, 'What the hell, I'll give it a shot.'"

The cop and engineer both had a good laugh. There was a knock at the door and another police officer came in to join his colleague at the table, taking the last hard chair next to the first cop. The first cop and the engineer stopped laughing.

"I told her you don't want an award or any silly public fanfare," said the second cop to the engineer. "But I said you're happy to meet her and receive a quick and quiet 'Thank you' from her, as she asked for. She's on her way in shortly, then we can go meet with her in the main office."

"I don't know what to say to her," said the engineer, addressing both cops. "What can you tell her, really?"

"It's tough," said the second cop. "It's never an accident. Maybe one in a hundred. Maybe if you're drunk and pass out on the track or something. But even then, what in the hell were you thinking being there, in proximity like that?"

"Is it always the same?" asked the first cop. "I mean, do they look the same, act the same?"

"Yeah, I wonder about the thinking and the looking," said the engineer. "They are the same. They stand there, straight up and tall, looking at the engine with no emotion, eyes open even as it approaches, and they know it ain't slowing down one little bit. It's not even a possible option at that point, and he knows it full well."

All three paused and looked down at the scuffed-up metal tabletop.

"At night, you can see the glow of the deer eyes, and same with the varmints running around, a fox or possum or whatever, back into the ditch," continued the engineer. "But not a man. The light hits them, and that's as far off as you can see them—not that far at all. You've got to let the horn go when you know it's him, yet you know at that same instant that he knows you're coming, and you know he ain't moving. He's thinking his last thoughts, accepting it...Jesus, he's asking for it. Each one of them would have a different state of mind—a different condition, of course—but they all look the same, staring up at you like that."

"He's actually looking right at you, past the engine and light?" said the second cop, asking in amazement. "You'd think the bright light alone plus the rumbling noise would throw him off, at least a bit."

"Right at you," said the engineer, attesting to the events, the scenarios. "The first one I hit, I saw the pearly whites of his eyes, looking up towards mine. Same with the second one...last thing I wanted to do was re-live that experience, but it was a year or so earlier and it was so surreal it was as though it hadn't happened, just some messed up nightmare. And so, I saw the whites of his eyes again. Day or night, you see his eyes. Since then, I let the whistle go, throw on the brakes, and at a certain distance, you have to just turn around and look away."

"Holy shit," said the first cop, astounded. "Unbelievable. You'd need your own therapy after seeing that. But I see now why you'd use your gun. It makes total sense, at least to give it a try, maybe find an innovative solution or something."

"Yeah, I didn't want to feel so helpless, the next time it happened," said the engineer. "Which I knew it inevitably would happen again—as I say that after the first eight times, Mr. Prescient Prophet here. So I thought I'd come prepared for the next round—hopefully the final round."

"He told me about it," said the second cop, about his colleague, the first cop. "But tell me if you wouldn't mind, firsthand, how did it all go down like that, in a nutshell?"

"Well, we were just chatting about how it all started, with me taking the gun on board," said the engineer. "I'd done it with some deer, out the window or door, day or night. That's why I took it along, to have some fun and, what the hell, right? In truth, I never really conceived of using it on a person, but like I say, I wanted to be prepared, in case...

"The last few times, I'd looked away. And I thought for going forward, once I'd hit some deer and had some practice, I thought, 'no you ain't, you son of a bitch,' and decided to give it a shot. I didn't even bother to think about his reaction. With deer, it's the sound of the shot, and then getting hit, of course—they're gone, running off into the ditch and beyond, regardless of the hypnotic state and stare. But the zombie stupor man...he'd already made his decision and locked it in, rationally or not."

The engineer took a deep breath...

"It was daytime, last week, as you well know. He stood there staring at me, out of town. And so, I grabbed the gun, cracked the door, leaned out, and I let her go. I was having a good day before I saw him standing there, so I got angry—I was pissed. I sprayed him, fast and hard. Fired a few first shots to get myself comfortable, then I let loose and fired as quick as I could, rounds going out so fast as if it was almost an automatic weapon. I hit him all over, up and down, from head to toe. Actually, toe to head—if you shoot at his feet along the ground, you quickly figure out your aim and trajectory. That's important when the train is still rolling along. I worked my way up his body, getting to his head and face in short order. I didn't hesitate on thoughts that I might blind him by accident, as what he was looking for was so much worse, obviously—at least I figured as much."

"Good lord," said the second cop, getting the story first-hand for the first time, as he rested his elbows on the table, looking like a child being told a new and fantastical fairy story. "So how long was he able to stand there and take it all like that, before going down?"

"Well, everywhere it hits you it has a different

sensation," said the engineer. "At first, when the rounds hit the aggregate and ties and steel track in front of him, he probably thought, 'What the hell is this?' He could handle taking his own life, but not the chaos of these shots, the whole circumstance as baffling as it would seem. His hypnotic state snapped—he had to have wondered...and then the legs get it, jitters running through his nerves in the thighs, tingles on the kneecaps. The stomach and torso stings, the balls, well...by the time they'd moved up his chest to his neck, he was off-balance, and you'd have a real tough time standing there if it hit your Adam's apple, after taking a few in the sack, right? He raised his arms to try and protect himself from the onslaught, almost as if completely forgetting the train that was barreling down on him, focusing on the even more immediate threat at hand, if only a difference of a mere few seconds. He went there to get the train, but he got something else altogether."

They all paused for a few seconds in disbelief before the engineer carried on and finished his story.

"As I got closer and he was off kilter and quite surprised, I sprayed his head and quickly back to his body, to get him to drop his guard. I did this back and forth, like a boxer hitting the bag in a mock sparring...but with skill, not like a stupid goddamned deer or something. Anyways, I think one hit his neck and then his nose, and he's struggling with the stings from the welts all over, and then his breath gets hit and he's winded, and now he's blinded by the splatter from a few of the head shots. And he jumped right off, with maybe three or four seconds to spare, at most. He tripped on the railway as he jumped and went tumbling right down into the ditch, somersault after cartwheel, rolling into the weeds and scrub and trash down there, cushioned by the prickly burrs.

"I slowed down and the train stopped within another minute or two, as I'd already hit the brakes when I saw him and grabbed the gun. Plus I wasn't going near top speed on exiting town, having just put that train together in the yard. I called you guys when it started to slow down, and before it stopped. When I started shooting, one part of me wanted to save him, but one part of me didn't give two shits if he did it or not. I was pissed off he did it on my time, in front of me. I figured he'd either take the shots and keep standing since he'd made the life decision prior to the shelling, or I thought maybe he'd just go find a bridge or a rope or a real gun—something else, to do it by another means."

"But he didn't," said the first cop, interrupting the engineer to finish the story himself. "He shook and dusted himself off and walked right back towards town. He met us on the road into the rail yard, and came with us, as simple as that."

"And he looked like a fucking Smurf when they walked him in here," said the second cop. "Unreal. Also, you have us re-thinking several of our own tactics because of your good deed, interesting as it was. Maybe you should give up the railway business and join us coppers."

They all looked at each other again, with gentle smiles. There was another knock at the door, and a third police officer walked in. He closed the door behind him and stood next to the table on the one vacant side of it.

"She's here," he said. "The poor wife is ready to thank her Good Samaritan train driver sniper hero, for keeping him together."

"How is she?" asked the first cop.

It was a question each one of them had wanted to ask.

"Well," said the third cop, taking his time to ensure he answered with the correct words. "She's a bit teary-eyed, rightly so. But she's a strong lady. She's got him in therapy and getting some help now. It seems they had a few financial problems, and maybe some marital problems, but nothing major...not insurmountable. He's not a goddamn nutter or anything, just some problems, like all of us have. He had a bad day or week and took it a bit too far, to be sure, but our good locomotive operator here saved the day...all with some fun choo-choo shoot 'em up action."

The engineer and the three cops nodded to one another in a positive agreement, offering reassuring looks and concluding smiles.

"Well, all's well that ends well," said the engineer, rising slowly from his chair, resting his hands on the table for leverage and balance as he got up. "If it just ends with some paintball."

# A Flat Tire Fire

Notwithstanding the painfully slow drive to town on the little spare tire, I arrived at the garage a few minutes before it was to open. The highway was already bustling with trucks early in the morning, on the approaches into and out of town, racing about in both directions. Many of the trucks were loaded with lumber, packaged up in thick white and indigo plastic wrap, heading south to catch the train. There were also empty trucks going the other way, heading back up north to collect more of these packages from the mills. This was a sort of border country here, between the dense forest and open prairie, with trucks hauling grain and cattle to the south, and modified flatbeds bringing fresh logs out of the bush from the north.

Knowing exactly where I was going from having driven right by it with my spare tire on the night before, I entered the town and drove through the bay of gas pumps to view the shop—Kenny's Tire Shop. Seeing no one was in yet, with the illuminated red light of the 'Open' sign still asleep, I circled around the bay and reversed my car into a parking spot, with the nose facing directly towards the garage door for an easy entry when Kenny opened up his shop.

I looked at that huge garage door and down to the clock on the dash as it ticked ahead from 6:58 to 6:59, in the a.m. The clock was slow, but no sooner had those few seconds passed when a man walked right beside the car, coming out from somewhere behind it. I hadn't seen him approach in the rearview mirror, but I assumed he had walked through the residential neighbourhood from home, then through the school playground adjacent to this parking space at his garage. It appeared he was somewhat off schedule, although characteristically or not, I couldn't tell. I felt like a spy, surreptitiously watching the movement of this man, and though I was certain he had noticed my vehicle sitting there and running, parked amongst the other more familiar longer-term parked cars and trucks here, he appeared focused in his beeline from his home to his business.

The man unlocked the door and went in, busying himself about in the front of the store section of the garage, by the cash register in the retail front windows which looked out to the gas pump bay, the bay located like an island between the shop and the rural highway. The red 'Open' light went on. I gave him another minute to organize himself and his business for the day, before proceeding in to conduct my more immediate business and ensuring I didn't get scooped by another like weary traveler or otherwise.

Once I was inside, I realized the man was already well back behind this convenience store-type of front of the gas station, presumably getting the garage and tire shop section organized as well. I could hear some clanging and banging about, so I just waited rather than going behind to accost and surprise him. Sure enough, he returned to the front within a minute or two.

"Hi, there," I said. "Kenny, is it?"

"Yeah," said Kenny, in an almost hostile or confrontational tone.

"Hi, I got a flat one out on the grid last night," I said. "Maybe a stone or grader blade or whatnot." I could already tell he didn't seem like the conversational type, but it might have just been this specific morning, so I figured there was no harm in offering him an affable possible explanation on the genesis of my flat tire, not that he would have needed the qualification to repair it.

"Yeah," said Kenny, again and without further questioning, in an odd and even more blunt matter-of-fact sort of way.

"Not sure if you can patch it up for me," I said, as I gave a cursory scan of the shop behind him. "Or if I need a new one, or something."

"Right," said Kenny.

"I wanted to be in here first thing, as our family has to head out—we're leaving the farm today with a pretty long trip back," I said, as if I had to try to elucidate some level of further detail on why I was there and what I wanted done.

"Drive it on in then," said Kenny, as if it was obvious I should have already done that. He trudged back through to the shop, over to where he could press the opener button for the big garage door.

I walked back with him, following him right to and then out the garage door, straight towards my car, already pointed in the right direction. I pulled ahead, entering the shop. It didn't appear he was paying any attention, so I stopped where I thought it made sense, popped the hatch, and walked right back around to take out the dirty flat tire, now wanting to expedite the process as much as I was able to.

"Oh, yeah," he said, looking at it while rotating the tire. Then he took it away, without an explanation or answer to my original question as to the status of the tire, back to his workbench-type of area, which was in front of the car and a bit off to the side, running along a long wall of tools that hung from nails and hooks set in sheets of plywood affixed to said wall.

There were tires stacked all over the garage, piled randomly on the floor in towers, on gigantic almost Costco-like shelves, and all about. There were tires for farm equipment, semis and other large trucks, some of them were new but dusty—they didn't appear particularly organized to a mere civilian like myself, but it seemed as though he probably did have a system of organization that was all his own, not unlike those folks with messy desks and scattered offices, only with tires, tools, and related tire fixing infrastructure everywhere, instead of stacks of papers and office junk all over the workspace.

The shop wasn't filthy, and it wasn't pristine—not that one would expect that, or want it, or if it was even achievable in a tire shop. One corner of the garage floor was well swept and an impressive level of clean, while other sections looked thoroughly unclean, or at least quite dusty and grimy.

Kenny had the tire set up on the workbench now, preparing to do whatever it was he was about to do, although I figured at this point his course of action was going to be fixing this existing flat tire of mine. I busied myself with slowly taking my time in scanning all of these tire types, as if I was browsing bookshelves at the library, or more likely at the used bookshop. I had no idea what I was looking at, but I gave an effort in trying to read the brand names and labels on the tires that had them, which I gathered gave an explanation of the measurements of grooves, widths, diameters, winter versus summer, and such; other tires had nothing but a sticker with a barcode on them, which I assumed was to scan it to ensure alignment with the correct given wheel and whatever other parameters of a customer's tire needs for their mode of transportation.

"Coffee," said Kenny, his first proactive words of the morning, at least in the brief conversation he'd had with me, as his first and unknown customer of the day. "It's on there, grab a cup."

"Great, thank you," I said, wanting to appear gracious in light of his hospitality in the offering, and in his now opening up as he continued beavering away on the flat tire fix. "I can sure use a cup this morning."

As Kenny had left the garage door partially open, I walked about the shop and into the outside cool and misty air, and back and forth, in a relaxing pace.

"These look new," said Kenny, almost seeming confused that they were. "They new?"

"Yeah, they're pretty new," I said. "Less than a year, I'd say. They're only the second set on this car."

"It might void the warranty on that tire by me fixing it," said Kenny.

I thought about that for a couple of seconds, but the

premise of his idea didn't make any sense to me, although it might have just been me.

"Well, it's either a fix of that one, or a new tire altogether, isn't it?" I said, genuinely wondering if I was missing something. "So, either way, I need a good tire—I don't care if it's this one that gets fixed or a new one off of the shelf there."

My question was met with total silence, as Kenny turned around and proceeded with his prepping the work to fix the flat tire, carrying on without saying anything—it seemed we were back to where we began only a few minutes earlier.

"I drove on that donut at about forty the whole way," I said, pushing ahead with some idle conversation, seeing if I could elicit much of a response. "The whole time it felt like it was going to roll right off, and then the car would collapse entirely on the highway, grinding down the asphalt till it sparked and scraped to a stop on the road, or pushing it into the ditch, or into a building here in town or something."

"Heh, that's all bullshit," said Kenny, not quite laughing but nonetheless I was getting a bit of a rise out of him. "You can drive as fast as you damn well want on that donut—your speed doesn't matter. It's only if you get turning and swerving around, especially on the gravel. It won't do anything otherwise. I've seen rednecks and hillbillies drive on donuts for months, years even."

"Huh," I said, learning something from this expert in his field, but deciding I didn't have much to reply with, so considered it safer playing the silence card myself now for a bit, gaming out my next words.

"Here," said Kenny, getting my attention and tossing

me a small stone which I caught, noticing right away the sharp tip on it like an arrowhead, with sparkles from the piece of granite or quartz twinkling away as I twisted it under the bright shop light coming from the ceiling high above. "There's your problem, pierced straight through the tire, like a sniper bullet."

I held the guilty stone and strolled back outside, watching one of the lumber rigs from the north approach the first major turn and slow down at the entrance to the town. The truck driver activated his Jake brake, hearing it growl and echo as the semi slowed down and then passed in front of the gas pump bay on the highway out in front of the shop. I went back in through the half-open garage door again, sort of slowly popping in and out, killing time back and forth behind the back hatch of my car and the garage driveway. I was sipping my Styrofoam cup of coffee between the fresh but chilly air outside and contrasting it with the warmer air but now with the burning rubber and chemical smell of the work being done on the tire inside the garage, when I noticed Kenny seemed to be taking a break from the surgery he was performing on the tire.

"I heard about that terrible crash a while back," I said.

"Heh," said Kenny. "Yep."

"So, the truck driver hit the ice on that turn there?" I said, still standing near the garage door. I looked towards the southbound direction of the highway, at the spot where the truck had just passed through and was presently carrying on south, and looked back to Kenny at his workbench in his garage.

"There was no goddamned ice," said Kenny. "Not even a sniff of frost."

I struggled to read the tone of his silence that followed.

73

In one second, it felt as if he wanted to open up and tell the entire story—to share this story of the event that was uniquely his right here at this location, his side of the story if in fact there were differing opinions or not, or perhaps his side if in the form of a descriptive narration of a crazy fictionalized version of the story of some sort that took place right here. However, in the next second, it seemed as though he didn't want to tell it at all, as if he were deeply hurt by the events, victimized by it, an event that could have been even much worse than it ended up being. Or, in the next second, maybe it was more simply that he was tired, he'd had a bad night of booze or indigestion or impotence or other unfortunate events in his personal life, in close proximity but so far from this less than ethereal plane here at his shop, Kenny's Tire Shop, on this cool and early summer morning.

*But I'm here for business and I want to hear the story firsthand, so to hell with your hangover, disinterest, silence, hidden tears...* I thought.

"He was going really fast then, blowing the turn and rolling, or what?" I said, trying to somehow prompt him.

"Eighty-three miles an hour," said Kenny, slightly slowing down the pace of his work so he was able to look up and state this to me directly, eyeball to eyeball, enunciating each syllable, so matter-of-factly. "Cops said so."

"Jesus. In what—what's that, a fifty zone?"

"Was fifty then, at the time. Forty now."

"Damn," I said, taking a minute to process it, having now heard it directly from the mouth of the proprietor himself. "Unreal."

I stared at the highway for another few minutes as he

worked with a silence among us. The tire sat on the workbench as Kenny went about other tasks, before letting me know it was almost done setting and that he could ring me up. Knowing I was nearly on my way, I tried to refocus myself on that, heading back out front with him, paying the bill, then returning to the garage with him, as he quickly went to work on putting the repaired tire back on my vehicle.

"Well," I said, standing by the back wheel, looking out to the highway again, as Kenny crouched below with the torque wrench and lug nuts. "You got a nice new shop out of the deal."

"What?" said Kenny in a barking tone, but he may have not heard me as he was working and as another truck was passing by outside at the same time.

"This shop," I said, speaking up and reiterating my approval of the new building, his business. "It's a great new shop you've got here, the building and all."

"Christ," he said, grumbling in disgust, looking between me and the passing truck on the road. "There was nothing wrong with the old one."

I'd heard the story from my uncle and also from a friend, independent but basically identical versions of the incident. Both of them knew Kenny and recommended I take the tire there to him that morning, rather than attempting the longer journey to the larger town on our way back to the city, our ultimate destination. My uncle had shown me photos from the news at the time, and jogging my recollection was assisted by my friend, who had reminded me of the incident the evening before. It had happened two years ago, but in the earlier spring of that year as opposed to the brief period of summertime we were enjoying at present.

It occurred right around the same time of day that I was in for this tire fix of mine, first thing in the early morning, right when a few locals would often stop in for coffee at the shop before they each got on with their own days, respectively. As per Kenny's description of the trucker's speed, later confirmed by the official investigators, a fuel truck didn't even consider slowing down as he approached the community, losing complete control of his rig at the curve entering town from the north, tipping on the turn and slamming into it, Kenny's original tire shop, taking out the bay of gas pumps on the way into the garage.

The wayward truck, brimful of fuel (along with the chemicals and whatever else was in and around the shop), exploded, blasting and burning the entirety except for Kenny and the couple of his pals there with him that morning, the patrons and neighbours visiting along coffee row. They'd been miraculously shielded from the explosion and saved by some large new tractor and combine tires that had been delivered the previous afternoon, and which Kenny had wanted to show them. If the group had been standing anywhere else in the vicinity, or said tires had not been delivered on time, they would have all been killed, melted away. However, and luckily, they got out, then stood on the other side of the highway, in the ditch across the road, and watched the shop go up in flames, the massive tire fire then blazing on for hours and hours into the afternoon...

Kenny tossed the spare tire—the so-called "donut" I'd driven in on—and the accompanying factory key into my hatch before slamming it back down.

"Check your nuts every fifty miles," said Kenny, then took the four or five steps from my hatch over to his garage door button, putting his finger on it as a signal that he wanted me on my way and out of there, so he could close it back down again and carry on with his day.

I reversed my car back out of the garage and into the original parking spot where I'd been waiting earlier that morning on my arrival, and then I put it in drive. As I inched forward towards the new bay of gas pumps, I gave Kenny a wave and in return I received a nod of the head. I could hear the loud chain from the garage as it pulled the door back closed again, which I took as my cue and put up my own driver's side door window.

I rolled my car away from the shop and slowly up to the stop sign, when, about to pull onto the highway, I saw the semi-trailer moving towards me, barreling along much quicker than it should have been going. Looking back through the rearview mirror at Kenny's shop, I decided it prudent to wait for the truck to pass by before getting back onto the southbound highway myself. I also decided that for the remaining few minutes where I would still be there within the town limits, I had no plans on exceeding that posted speed limit sign of forty.

# The Hike

On the surface of the middle of the lake, the ferry continued making its way through the storm, heading back towards town, tossing around on the rough whitecaps in the wind, nearly out of view behind the pines and cedars on the point. When the lightning hit the first boat, it was as if a giant birthday cake sparkler went off, igniting the icing into a systemically engulfed blaze of dessert, afloat.

Luke and Matt looked at each other in dread, sickened by the carnage all around them. The minor beach and simple boat launch had been turned into a hopeless war zone, an apocalyptic scene. While considering if the magnitude of hail could be measured as an analogy to bowling balls, they looked back out to view the sun and baby blue sky peeking out from beyond the mountain across the lake, where they could see the end of the storm, the peace approaching in good time even if not soon enough.

**2:33 p.m.**

Hail (now the size and strength of softballs) hit the ground and trees, exploding icy and slushy shrapnel all about, with heaps of unblended plain snow cone covering the frosty white ground. Higher branches snapped off, leaves pulverized. Large chunks of wood from the dock were chiseled away, boards broken up. A seagull dropped from the sky onto their former log bench, its head covered in a ball of ice, the hail forming a sort of ironic helmet on the dead bird.

A tourist stuck his head out from behind a tree to sneak a look, allowing an unfortunate opening for hail to smash his face, knocking him out cold, maybe forever. Others were moaning and screeching, taking grapefruit-sized hail (or at least the razor-like shards of it) on their exposed skin unprotected by the trees, breaking bones, leaving giant crimson gashes. The older lady and one of the Japanese students under their former tree were both wailing, holding their own bloodied arms and heads, attempting to protect and mend.

"Get ready," said Luke, once again trying to direct the exposed and ignorant tourist-hikers, but his scream was still inaudible. Luke and Matt snuggled up to the trunk at the best available angle, kissed the mossy bark, and covered their heads with their arms as a last line of defense.

The centre of the storm neared, wreaking havoc all around them. The water began to splash, as if shot-puts were being tossed in from the shore, or the lake was starting to boil. But it was the hail, now larger than baseballs. It moved from the lake onto the beach, hitting the sand like an artillery shelling on a doomed Normandy beach on D-Day.

"Look across the lake, up top," said Matt, also yelling, and pointing. "The blue sky and sun, that's it. You can see the end of it."

The dead calm atmosphere of mere minutes ago now saw a consistent gale with extreme gusts, blowing and bending all types of trees, from jack pines to firs, twisting them around as if they were the greens of carrot tops. The thick dark slate-cappuccino cloud was moving so fast and hung so low they could feel the agitation and roll, even as they hunkered down at the base of the large trees.

"Get in tighter," said Luke, yelling as loudly as he could, pointing and directing the unprotected to a safer spot. "Under those branches, hug the trunk." They could hear him scream, but the words were indecipherable. Yet, organically, they did just that, moving in close, hugging the trees—tree-huggers or not.

**2:28 p.m.**

The first "ouch" quickly became one of many yelps, then shrieks. They were somewhat of horror and of an actual physical pain, as if the hikers were standing in a firing line and taking shots from a paintball or BB gun (in fully automatic mode, at point blank range) to their exposed skin in nervy parts.

"Ow, Christ!" said someone, as it rang out from behind a nearby tree. It was one of the tourist hikers, his phone taking a direct hit from the hail and shattering, the hail now larger than peas, like gumballs. He kept screaming, shaking his hand in pain and disbelief from under his branch.

The brothers scanned the beach and looked towards the lake, watching the hail come down, longing for a picnic table shield or outhouse bunker, but no such protection existed. The hail started as small as bird shot, becoming like pearl barley, then the size of peas, all within a minute. Phone cameras were out, snapping pictures and video of the blizzard and wintery-looking ground from all angles. There was an odd tension behind each screen, like a feeling between a rare exotic experience that must be fully taken in and enjoyed, as if a unicorn had landed in their midst on the beach; it was contrasted with a reasonable fear of terror, as if a comprehensive and epic natural disaster was imminent in the lightning and hail storm already starting to pound them.

They ran out from their tree on the beach, doing a parallel sprint, with hands up to protect their faces as if boxing, hurdling the log and taking cover in an improved position, they thought. They looked back to their former shelter, as an elderly couple and some Japanese college students were taking it over, right as the snowflakes and ice pellets merged and transformed into hail.

"Right there, let's go," said Matt, looking for a break that was not coming, ordering his brother with a hand signal and shout. "Now!"

Matt was thinking the same thing, eyeing a massive evergreen surrounded by huge cedars and redwoods, just off the beach and into the woods, right behind their enormous log bench.

"That won't last," said Luke, becoming concerned

himself on where this storm was headed, but he had a good idea even if he did not know exactly. "Let's find a better tree. That cloud and all that sleet and whatever coming down... It's only going to get worse."

**2:22 p.m.**

The hikers seemed relieved the downpour was dissipating, while at the same time the tourists among them were fascinated by the phenomenon of snow and ice...and in the middle of summer. Concern remained on the ominous cloud continuing to gain steam in its churn, removing the sun as it now filled in the entire sky, resulting in a significant drop in temperature and arctic blast for the soaked individuals waiting on the beach. While graced with a brief reprieve on the beach, it was also clear there was precipitation in many forms all around them and that it was intensifying, even during the short amnesty.

"If not that, the snow sure will," said Matt, reaching out his arm again, exposing it to the lightening rain and emerging mini snowflakes, with even tinier ice crystals and pellets now coming down in the mix.

Lightning and thunder flashed and cracked together every few seconds as the temperature plummeted. Seagulls flew overhead in a chaotic frenzy, as if they had lost their way, or did not even know where they had come from or where they were going to begin with, their radar scrambled.

"It's getting cold," said Luke, grinning. "That chill might jolt some of these southern and foreign folks more than the storm will."

They stood under a thick spruce, being sheltered

somewhat by the lower branches and being close to the wide trunk. A lucky few of the universally well-prepared hikers pulled umbrellas and raincoats from their bags, while those who came prepared for today's forecast of significant heat and sunny sapphire skies relied on their sundry hats and random tree branches.

"There it is," said Matt, as the intensity of the precipitation grew by the second, from a light sprinkle to a seeming monsoon rain within a couple of minutes at most. "Let's get under that tree."

Simultaneous with a crashing bang, another lightning flash hit the mountain across the lake, this time striking a cluster of trees and starting a fire, easily visible from their position. The fire managed to burn on even in the heavy downpour. The cloud of grey and chestnut roiled in what looked like a soft spin as the cloud passed over the mountain. It moved west and sank lower, hovering over the lake and descending towards the beach, where the hikers from the second and third boats waited patiently for their return ferry rides back to town.

**2:16 p.m.**

"No, look at the water," said Luke, also chortling while pointing to the surface of the lake beyond the boat. "Any second now and they'll be totally soaked."

"Yep, those folks on top of the boat are going to get it good," said Matt, snickering. "They're headed right into it, unless they can get across in time."

"Yeah," said Luke, considering the level of precipitation. "That sprinkle is going to turn heavy any second. Look at that cloud move. It looks like a nebula."

"And there comes the rain," said Matt, putting out his arm to feel with certainty that it was starting to come down, as gently as a bathroom shower with feeble water pressure moving through lazy pipes.

"Yikes," said Luke, looking at his stoic brother and the more concerned tourists scattered about.

**2:09 p.m.**

As the boat left the dock, lightning struck the mountain across the lake, creating an explosive spark as it hit the Precambrian rock on the side, sending an instant and constant thin stream of smoke straight up into the sky until the billowing grey plume blended in with the dark cloud that was advancing. The accompanying thunder came within a split second of the flash; those on the beach felt the powerful concussion, as many were covering up their ears.

"Damn, I thought we'd make that first boat. Oh well," said Matt, sipping his water bottle and rationing the drink, knowing they were going to be sitting for some time, and the harsh sun they had battled all day on the hike might return at any moment. "Better to sit here on the beach with these lovely Japanese ladies than on boat number one with those wise old early-riser folks. You don't even want to be on that boat...too stout to float," said Matt, trying to lighten the mood during their long wait by cracking jokes of attempted justification.

Resigned, Luke and Matt went back to the beach and sat on a massive redwood log laid out across the sand, as if a border between the beach and the dense forest to their backs.

**2:05 p.m.**

"Sorry, guys," said the ticket taker on the dock, offering an apologetic smile to Luke and Matt. "We've got to let the guests from the first boat on first, then the second if there's any room. But we're at capacity now and will have to get going. You gents will have to wait until at least the next boat, if not the third one, which is yours, the original boat you took. The next one comes in about an hour. I'm sure you'll make that one, as many from the first two don't make it down till the end of the day, not nearly as quick as you boys are, enjoying their stroll in nature more."

**2:03 p.m.**

It took them only another fifteen minutes to complete the descent. Returning to the beach right as some hikers from the first boat trip out (from the early dawn morning run) had indeed made it back in time. They stood in the long line on the dock waiting to board the ferry, watching a thick dark antique pewter cloud begin to blot out the sun as it made its way over the mountain directly across the lake.

**1:48 p.m.**

"I can see the lake, right through those trees," said Matt, pointing the way as he was longing for a chair and a beer. "We'll make that first boat. There's no way all those fossils will make it back in time."

They walked through the much cooler thick foliage, where the ferns and like plants were brushing their damp fronds against the legs of Luke and Matt.

"Oh, man," said Luke, walking down under an emerald canopy that was creating a pleasant and shady defense from the searing sun and accompanying heat. "You can feel the sunburn when you get out of the direct rays. Amazing."

The hikers rubbed their brows, taking a final look back up the mountain (viewing the alpine meadow near the peak, where they, not even two hours ago, had a smoke and a snack, then turned back around) before heading down for the home stretch to where they had moored in the late morning.

"Good," said Matt, trying to catch his breath, joining his brother. "My neck and arms are fried...look how red they are. Man, I'm dehydrated, too. I've got sunstroke or something coming on. I'm like a freaking lobster with heat exhaustion. We've got to get out of this sun..."

Luke stood on the exposed path of dusty shale and smooth slate, right as the open trail met the hemlock forest. The zone of evergreen soon merged into a rainforest, and after only a few steep reverse switchbacks down, the brothers would make it back to the beach, their day-long hike complete.

"And this is it, the last of that brutal sun. We're going straight down now, right towards the lake," said Luke, combing his sweaty fingers through his drenched hair, waiting for his tired and struggling brother to catch up. "I bet we'll make that first boat, no problem."

**1:37 p.m.**

# First Born, Last Ghost

"I'm coming," Frank said, smiling even as his eyes began to well up. "I'll be joining you real soon, love. We'll finally be together again..."

He looked down to the shining coral granite monument, slamming the old spade into the adjacent rock-like dirt on the right side of the family plot. On a metallic echo, as if hitting concrete, the implement slipped from his grip, bounced back up, the handle hitting him in the mouth, cutting his lower lip.

"Goddamn," Frank said, screaming to himself. He dabbed his lip with his palm to check the damage. "Christ's sake."

Frank looked down and could not even see a scuff in the soil from his effort, only the round dollop and twisty streak of blood on his hand, from his lip. He tried again. This time, he gripped the handle of the spade, angling the blade in the solid dirt right at the position of where he wanted to dig. Frank put his foot on it, pushing his leg into the tool with as much force as he was able to, lifting his other leg up for leverage in the process. The shovel did not move. He slipped off, clenching the shaft to maintain his balance, safely landing, feet back on the ground.

Now steady, Frank gave a pat to his cut lip once more, rubbing his sweaty and dusty brow, looking back towards his house and the town site across the highway from his house—the town that once was, but was no more. He looked back down to where he stood on his plot, where he had tried to dig. Resigned, he leaned down on one knee, kissed his scarlet blood-smudged and dirt-stained hand, placing his ochre palm out with his fingers spread on the firm soil. Frank ran his hand across the stone, touching each etched letter of her name.

Getting hold of the handle of the shovel in his right hand and picking up the shotgun with his left, Frank took his time with calculated paces, ambling back to his worn pickup truck parked aslant the cemetery gate.

He began to drive the three miles back to his farmhouse. Halfway along, in a perfect cliché even if however ludicrous, a ball of some dried-out kochia drifted along in the breeze of dust, blowing from a field of summerfallow directly across the road and near the empty town site. Looking further ahead and on his side of the road (just beyond the ditch and no doubt from where the tumbleweed had originated), a coyote was trotting next to the exterior hedgerow of Frank's yard.

"I guess the coyote would've smelled it," Frank said, considering the would-be outcome. "Bad plan. Oh, well. I've got a new plan, foolproof. A final one."

\*

Turning off the highway, Frank parked at the entrance of the road into his yard, further back from the house than his regular spot. He took the gun and grabbed a jerry can out of the box of the truck, leaving the shovel behind. He started at the deteriorating steps, slowly circling the house, carefully pouring a thin stream of gasoline onto the wooden clapboard façade above the foundation. Inevitably spilling some on the foot-high grasses and weeds growing around the base, Frank completed the square back at the verandah where he had started, dribbling out the last few drops, emptying the container as he climbed up to the top step.

Frank went inside and got himself a much-needed rye. As he poured the drink, he smelled the gasoline residue on his hands. He washed his hands over the kitchen sink, struggling between the faucet and teeming pile of dirty dishes. Frank walked back out to the verandah and sat down, resting his arms and hands on his beloved hand-made cedar-stained Adirondack. He set the whisky down, picking up the gun beside the chair and setting it across his lap, as if preparing to defend the home from would-be intruders peering out of the caraganas, if not zombies making their way here from the graveyard he had just visited, those past and soon-to-be reunited neighbours. Frank reached into the front pocket of his ratty teal plaid shirt and took out a vinyl pouch of tobacco, a book of loose wrappers, and a disposable lighter of an orangey-gingerish-like colour.

Frank stared across the road to the town site as he lit the freshly rolled cigarette, taking one long drag, maintaining the smoke deep within his lungs for several seconds, exhaling a disjointed oval ring from his cracked lips before releasing the remaining plume of exhaust out his nose. He took another sip of whisky.

A grid road went south off the highway, directly aligned with Frank's road on the north side. The gravel concession was the main entrance to the town for decades, now only serving as a side road to farms and some new wells serviced by a gas company, operators of both being based in the city seventy miles away.

"No one not from around here would have any idea a town used to stand there," Frank said, speaking aloud to himself as he slowly considered this obvious fact among his other related even if jumbled nostalgic thoughts.

*

The last trace of the town was a decaying home overgrown on all sides with caraganas and lilacs. The house was abandoned more than a decade ago and demolished last week. Frank watched them bulldoze and torch the site from the same seat as he was resting in now. The patch of ploughed over earth would be seeded next spring; the entirety of the old town would be a golden field of wheat or barley ready for harvest at this time next year. It would be taken off by he who owned and ran it now, some modern grower from the city.

"The town isn't even a ghost town now," Frank said, taking another drag and puff. "Ghost field, maybe. Jesus."

Frank's son and grandson lived in the city, too. They, too, farmed Frank's land now, although Frank still tinkered. He remained active until only two years ago when something went wrong in his head: he thought he was braking but somehow got the ATV going full throttle in reverse down a bunny hill in the field, hitting a badger hole and rolling the quad on top of himself, twisting all his joints the wrong way. He should have been dead, as most are in such situations, but he did not even break a bone, only bruises managing to display all colours of the ROYGBIV spectrum. Recovery of his knees, ankles, elbows, and shoulders took time; and there was the head issue, whatever that was...

At that point, Frank did not fight his son and grandson as they took full control of the operations, as other survivors might; he was welcoming, blessing it.

His son and family were at their own home in the city this weekend, with all generations taking part in the festivities on the anniversary of the founding of that city. Next weekend, they were scheduled to come out to the farm and celebrate another anniversary: Frank's ninetieth birthday. It was agreed that that would be it for Frank living on his farm, and he would abandon the good ship homestead, retreating to the 24/7 premium service and finest comforts of a new home: the home. A move to the home of sunsets, in the season of death. Some retirement or seniors or nursing home was not his home; his true home was here.

As with the city, the village/town/hamlet/ghost town across the road was incorporated ninety years ago next weekend. It came to be the day after Frank was born, in the same location. Every town along the railway right-of-way was founded then, give or take a year or two. Each one grew, year by year, some boomed, some busted...some died. The gamut of the good, bad, and ugly of local industries, wars, leaders, cultures, farming practices, etc.

Then the rail line became a branch line, then an

unused spur, then the railway company abandoned it, then some farmers turned railway men, then the steel track and wooden ties got ripped up and carted off with the aggregate, then the quackgrass grew; then the Grasshopper Pacific Express was all that remained.

Some of the towns were true ghost towns now: foundations and various ruins sat decaying, visibly. But Frank's town was no more, in each and any possible sense. The town grew during his first twenty years, then it slid slowly into nothingness. The descent began as early as in the Great Depression when some of the first settlers lost their farms during the Dustbowl, the natural population decline in the second war, farms that did not go under became larger, mechanized, and more efficient, and then the local plant shut down: the nail entering the coffin.

With each subsequent hammering down on that final nail, houses, businesses, the school, churches, and grain elevators followed. The great leap backward was underway. Even the cemetery: the grave of Frank's wife was the freshest one, laid to RIP there nearly twenty years ago. Back around that time, there were still a few occupied houses in town, a church, a wooden elevator, and a nothing hotel although with a bar. A much nicer hotel and modern restaurant opened up down the road in the last real town in the area; this killed theirs. The other holdouts, the elderly people, they kept on moving to the city and kept dying. The homesteaders were re-settling, underground and back to nature.

\*

Frank looked nearer, within his own yard. He was

surrounded by the remnants of his own war with nature, from this past summer, the one before, the previous few. He was not tending to the cows in the pasture, pigs in the barn, nor crops in the field any longer. And so, he tried to keep himself busy with other hobbies; putter about with projects he had thought about years ago, but put off, for far too long:

There was the magpie trap of a baited box and chicken wire, with ineffective rusty mechanism.

There was the fishing line tied to a cinder block, a piece of popcorn embedded in the hook for a hungry and unsuspecting movie-going crow.

There were the fake wasp nests hanging, topped up with cola, long gone flat.

There was the burning barrel for smudges, sitting under the sturdy shamrock green elm tree to gas the fleeting, fluttery lime green Peter Pan-like aphids.

There was the ant hill doused in powdered laundry detergent and lemon peels, with pods of poison placed on the periphery.

There was the snare over the gopher hole, with the garden tool implement for a fun game of whack-a-mole after the soft noosing.

There was the off-kilter bug zapper next to the flagpole, transforming mosquitos into fireflies deep into the night, if for only one bright second.

Frank looked around the verandah floor where he saw the arsenal of his messy war with nature: cans of sprays and drops and foams, an ancient fly swatter, pillars of citronella candles, traditional and new sticky mouse traps, pesticides, herbicides (*flipping dandelions*, Frank thought), fungicides ("goddamn black knot dog shit on a stick in my trees," Frank said), containers of borax and others of warfarin, a BB rifle, a pellet pistol, a crossbow, a rifle and a pistol (both of the .22 LR), axes and shovels. And an inbred black farm cat slept on the Adirondack next to Frank, the one vacated by his dear wife now many years ago.

\*

Frank took another breath of fresh air from his cigarette and another sip of elixir from his glass. He looked down to the shotgun on his lap, patting the stock and stroking the barrel. He took the lighter out of his pocket, and again leaned down on his bended knee as he had at the cemetery. He got to the angle where he was able to tilt the lighter and allow the flicker of flame to touch the last drop of gasoline. Not yet evaporated, it ignited, starting on fire quickly, advancing to the adjacent drop, other drops, heading down the steps as the drops became a line, a stream, then a clear path leading to the fork on the bottom step, where it took off and each flame rose up like knocked-down dominoes in reverse. He shooed the cat from the chair, who jumped through the railing and off into the furthest part of the yard, quickly making it to a truck by a weeping willow tree, where the cat stopped to turn around and view where it had just escaped from, with assistance. Frank backed onto the Adirondack, sitting down in as relaxed a position as he could, taking the last sip of his rye and the last drag of his smoke, while watching the flames dance around the house and climb up the front of the verandah.

He could feel the heat from the flames, becoming

warmer as the fire grew higher on the wood, rising up around the house. Frank tossed the lighter down the steps, the carrot-looking body merging with the blaze before generating a minor explosion. He flung the last of the cigarette butt into the flames. The fire grew closer to his feet, expanding its radius onto the wood that was not already doused in the accelerant. He chucked the whisky glass off the porch, straight into the fire. The flames rose above the verandah railing, reaching up as if trying to grab the eaves trough. The fire crackled and echoed from the four corners of the house, including from inside the open front door behind him, as the kitchen in the back side of the house was also now burning.

Frank looked through the wall of flame and across the road to his abandoned town, knowing the last ruin in proximity would soon disappear, completing its rise and fall. The grand nonagenarian party, for him and his town. The final un-incorporation. The return to nature.

"No cake, but we got us a hell of a candle," Frank said, as he picked up the shotgun. "We put in a good shift. Happy birthday to us!"

He noticed the streak of dried blood on his hand and thought of the cemetery and his love, promising he would be joining her real soon. He tried to look across the road to the town again, but it was now blurred by the heat haze mirage and real flame itself now fully enveloping the lower half of his house.

"Heh, I survived the cataracts," said Frank, smiling and chuckling. "And outlived the town. Our poor village, expired."

Frank thought of the town, strolling along the boardwalk with his young wife in their earliest of years, remembering the past to channel the future.

"Well, no use keeping the old girl waiting any longer then..."

# Shopping for Lisa, Part I: Love and Vanilla

Jolly me, I'm going to get some creamy eggnog, but then Lisa gives me this list with these clear instructions to obtain some key ingredients for a couple of fancy baking recipes she's going to make on Christmas Eve and then for dinner on Christmas Day. She thinks it'll be swell to invite some of the family over, from both sides, who'll then be fucked off by Boxing Day so we can have some cozy time together, alone for the rest of the holidays, a festive occasion.

I've never been in this store and don't even go to the city that often (let alone that area), but she's so keen on these high-end provisions that can't be bought anywhere else. She says, The items can't be found anywhere normal like a grocery store because the spices there are of a poor quality to begin with, going on saying, They're not processed right after sourcing them at origination, probably sitting on wholesale shelves and then in the shopping aisle for months, if not years—the entire supply chain seems to be a disaster, even if that's all I've ever known and the products all seem fine enough to me; spices don't go bad, I'm thinking.

She's raving on and on about the great quality of all the spices and such in this store, what amazing work they're doing in sourcing it all from farmers abroad without greasy middlemen, buying the products at a fair price and whatnot because they grew them all the right way like organic or something or other. I figure, maybe I'll grab some nutmeg there too, a great quality version of it if they have it, for the quintessential holiday rum and eggnog, down on the rug in front of the wood-burning fireplace, mistletoe overhead, once her family and mine have vacated—I'm nothing if not a romantic. Heh. That said, I know her dad is a fan of the drink, so I'll gain extra points from her and her old man on the Eve before the elaborate Christmas dinner, which won't hurt the cause.

The door jingles on entrance as I walk into this weathered century-old red brick building. Many aromas hit me in the nose like a jab from Tyson. I notice they've got this whimsical décor and big band music playing on a far-off speaker. There's a bronze tin ceiling with ornate floral patterns making it seem as if you're in a Paris restaurant, I'm imagining. The shop's organized like a pharmacy for the most part, but one in a museum. It also has pepper plants, growing bright tangerine ones, like fun-size hurricane-shaped pumpkins, in the window shelves and hanging pots. They're growing various herbs and spices that must be scalable or just for personal use, I'm thinking, maybe the aesthetic appeal drawing in customers with the seeming authenticity—how Lisa got sucked in, no doubt.

I see these short glass bottles of bitters and extracts to the left, kitchen gadgets and cook books on an island ahead, chilies and hot spices behind it, a smokeshow blonde female clerk standing measuring out spices at a table, packaging them on her own working island in the middle of the core spices racks. And so, I wander over there, noticing all kinds of pepper and salt, browsing through the colours and grinders, reading the descriptions in awe, but as if I knew what I was looking for, which was just plain black frigging regular pepper.

Walking up to me is this hipster clerk wearing a tight tattered forest green plaid flannel shirt, dark skinny jeans rolled up at bottom halfway up his shin, shiny black boots as if he was a soldier, covered in facial hair with a beard that kept going like he'd been in a cave in Afghanistan without a razor for decades, a pine green fedora, horn rim glasses—you get the picture.

I say to this guy, I just need some pepper and a few other spices I have a list for, supplies for the gal's Christmas baking, seasonal cocktails and the like, which seems obvious enough to me.

## PINK IS THE NEW BLACK (PEPPER)

But this clerk then walks me over to where the pepper was and asks, What kind of pepper do you want? I say, I want black pepper, like he doesn't understand me, this dolt all dressed up like a toff from some other strange galaxy. He says, Well, there are all kinds of peppers, and he starts explaining them all, pointing them out on this shelf which only had pepper on it. Many kinds of pepper—I could see out the corner of my eye that salt had its own shelf too, one over. He's taking sample jars to show me how they smell and what you can do with each kind for cooking and the like, talking all formal-like. Pepper: green, red, pink, white, several kinds of black of course, then there were mixes of multi-colour peppercorns and some with herbs and spices all in a single jar. Blends of these peppers. Some ground, some whole like a waiter grinds up at a fancy restaurant. Pepper and salt had their own shelves, sharing this long wall to the right when you walk in the door. I can't believe it, nor this hipster clerk.

I sort of brush him off a bit and say, Look, I only want regular black pepper so whatever here is closest to that is what I want, I don't know what all this other stuff is and don't care, bud. He says, Well, sometimes you need to know what you want for the nuance in the flavour of whatever dish you're cooking. I look at him like, Duh, and are you going to sell me some freaking pepper now or what?

I think that throws him off a bit, so he goes and says something more interesting: black pepper is a stimulant. That gets my attention, it sure does. He says, It speeds up the body's energy and pace of metabolism, driving the production and increasing endorphins and serotonin in your brain, affecting anxiety and insomnia and whatever else up top you got going on in the noggin. He says, It's like coffee kind of, but much better.

He's got me thinking a bit about it, as I'm standing there looking at this ridiculous selection of peppers, I'm thinking, maybe each kind has a different effect as a stimulant, and maybe I should ask him, since he's so excited by it all. But then he jumps right on to ask what else I'm after on my Lisa's spice shop shopping list. Of course, she's written down all these blends she wants me to get, like a fish blend, stew blend, stuffing mix, Scarborough Fair, but didn't put down a specific pepper, just pepper. Well, Malabar pepper is what that turns out to be, if you ever find yourself in such a situation, wondering about basic pepper. The bohemian shopman sells me on the premium version of that, called Tellicherry, because I'm thinking, only the best for my Lisa, 'tis the season. Then he sells me on a four-colour blend, which has that jet black one plus the dark green, white, and pink, which looks like punch or watermelon to me—he says, The magenta adds a nuanced sweet fruit flavour to your dishes and looks Christmasy enough on the table, which I can't disagree with, looking for extra points from both Lisa and her family as I am.

Anyway, ask for Tellicherry, if you ever get the chance, as if you're some sort of pepper connoisseur, to impress.

**EVERYTHING NICE IN SPICE**

The clerk asks me, What else? I tell him, I don't know, like vanilla and cinnamon and whatever, as I'm looking at this crumpled up list from the Post-It note in my pocket trying to confirm what was on there, these single ingredient items plus the blends, for all her holiday cooking things, baking, her recipes. Plus, let's not forget my eggnog, most important—the regular grocery store will have to suffice.

He walks me around the row of pepper and salt; they've got dozens of kinds of salt, a longer shelf on that wall than pepper, unto itself for some bleeping salt. Black lava Hawaiian salt, salmon looking Himalayan salt, coarse and ground into various sizes of salts, truffle celery garlic seasoning salt, Caesar salt, kosher salt. Salt, not just a random mineral, but from a mine and from the sea, specific seas in different regions. Dozens of flavours. Jesus, I tell you.

I didn't know what to expect in this store—it was starting to feel like a bazaar on the Silk Road or somewhere. But the clerk picks up one bottle of vanilla extract and he says, I assume this is what you want, or what she wants, for baking? I say, Fuck yeah, it's extract, not knowing if he was going to go on and on about something again. Instead he says, This is it, the only kind we get in from Tahiti, the best of the best. He says, There's some from Madagascar; total shit compared to this bottle. His voice goes up and he's almost emotional about this special South Sea vanilla, like out of body. I say, Great, thinking let's move on then with this personal shopper business and get the hell out of here.

Then his voice goes down to a whisper. He kind of leans in to speak in a softer tone and tells me, It contains something called piperonal—I have to ask him to repeat that a few times so I could remember how to pronounce it. Piperonal—piperonal. It also has some other name but whatever. And so, he tells me with this dainty beta goofball smirk of his that, piperonal has these aromatherapy traits which can improve your mood, reduce your stress and whatnot, just from its smell. I think, fine, but who frigging cares, right; his smile grows and he says, Get this, it promotes sexual arousal. This part of vanilla is like an antidepressant, relaxing you, and the stuff will make your girl horny—increases her libido! Can you believe it? Fucking vanilla. This funny douche is starting to grow on me now, I think. I ask, How, and he says, It's just the scent, so by all means let her bake away with the stuff, take in those fumes, baby. And those cakes and shit taste great too, so sign me up, right? I'm whiffing away, getting aroused myself thinking, it's a placebo effect or something, but either way I have to start thinking about baseball to calm down.

What else? he says. No wait, he says, running me around the measuring island handing me a jar called vanilla sugar. We recently put this one together, he says, for your gal's extra special baking, or even a dash in her coffee will get her going. He sprinkles a dash into my palm then his. I watch him lick it up and I follow suit. I'm kind of in a daze now, as if the extract sampler he made me smell then taste this vanilla sugar had made me a legitimate bit horny right there in the spice shop, making me think further about all I'm going to get now during the holidays. Merry Christmas to me, Lisa, and her cakes! A whole new appreciation for vanilla, a wholesome ingredient you'll never think the same about again.

**ONE TRUE CINNAMON**

I say, Oh shit, sorry, bud, sort of snapping out of my trance from the fragrance, all the thoughts of sex and vanilla. Cinnamon, I say. We need some cinnamon for the Christmas goodies. Baseball isn't working any longer, so I go to the bullpen—I'm trying to think of boring carols and snowmen like Frosty and other stupid things to tame my trousers.

The cinnamon is right there by the vanilla, a ledge atop an antique butterscotch desk or armoire or something. There're not dozens of cinnamons like salt and pepper. However, there are a few kinds, more than the one I would have assumed there was when walking into this shop. This clerk prick again asks, What kind of cinnamon do you want? Fuck's sake, like I know. If I don't know my pepper, how the hell am I going to know my cinnamon, I ask him. He shows me the cinnamon samplers and while I'm a bit pissed again with all this, to be honest, I'm a bit drawn into it now, so I let him have his way, enlightening me. I crack a few though, like he grabs the first mini jar and I say, Let me guess, that's the kind you use only for buns? I get a light chuckle out of him—it's all I'm after.

Cinnamon comes in a few different kinds. This stuff called cassia is from the same family but not proper cinnamon, if you follow. Cassia's more common, comes from China and Indonesia, it's caramelly, the most pedestrian crap you find in the grocery store. Heh, look at me, becoming a spice snob now! Vietnam or Saigon is the strongest, potent, a rusty colour, use it for candy and curry. Ha! Seriously though, what you want comes from Sri Lanka, the true cinnamon, a lighter tawny colour, more easygoing flavour, even if it's a bit complex. This is also your baking cinnamon, amazing stuff. The clerk says, It's a stimulant and sedative, not unlike vanilla, but the properties won't necessarily do anything for you in the sack, or your important effort in trying to get into the sack. What else can I help you find? he asks, wanting to move it along I figure, so good enough, as it was getting busy in the store by this point in my shopping spree.

## THIS IS YOUR BRAIN ON NUTMEG

I say, It looks like she needs nutmeg for baking, but even more important, I need it for my rum and eggnog, giving him a wink and a gentle elbow, not wanting to hurt this wimp. He says, Good call, it's great for Christmas baking, put it on the roast vegetables for the showy dinner, and of course the requisite eggnog. Then he floors me when he says, Do you know, you can get seriously high with nutmeg? Like not just sub-orbital, but true outer space high. It's quite hallucinogenic.

I'm thinking he might be ribbing me, as it seems so far-fetched. His look is dead serious as he starts to explain it all. Nutmeg is a stimulant, sedative, hallucinogenic. It's got these active ingredients having psychoactive properties.

He says, It's not just as a ground spice in some jar. The way you want nutmeg is to grind it up yourself by grating it, keeping the freshness to not lose the potency of the high. And so, he walks me over to the graters, or planers, then takes one of them over to where the jars of nutmeg were. Here they were, these balls like nuts and he takes one out of the sampler and starts grating it—the smell was incredible, like nutmeg, but unlike any nutmeg I'd ever smelt before. He starts talking away again, but not about different kinds of nutmeg because I guess there's only the one, but he whispers again like he did telling me vanilla makes chicks horny, and there he says again, You can get a real great high by eating nutmeg straight up, or mix it in something, whatever, man.

I say, What the hell are you talking about? I put it in my rum and eggnog during Christmas season and I get cheery like old Saint Nick, but that's from the drink, not from a trace of some trivial silly spice. He says, No, it's not only alcohol and weed, but you also need to be thinking about all the culinary kitchen spices in a serious way. The right chili peppers will make you sweat and then see things that aren't there. Wormwood makes your vision leave you. Poppy seeds will mess you up and throw your drug test off to a level as if you've been shooting heroin. Stay away from those bagels with the tiny black seeds. But I only want to mention the nutmeg here and now, this shocker...

He says, If you ingest nutmeg in larger amounts it leads to euphoria, a natural high, a great recreational drug in the spice cabinet. This guy is smiling away like a goddamn clown, then he frowns and warns, It can be most toxic if taken wrong. I learn it's a stimulant, but, he says, It has sedative properties, is a tremendous hallucinogenic, and it's even an aphrodisiac, if your vanilla isn't working for your gal. He pulls me over, a bit out of earshot of any other customers, going on this educational lecture almost, saying how nutmeg contains this compound or chemical or whatever called myristicin, is mind-altering if you take enough of it. One problem though is it can last some time, your high. It can really trip you out as much as acid even, the phenomenal hallucinogenic drug that nutmeg is. You really have to watch how much you're doing and pay close attention, as it doesn't kick in right away, so you truly don't want to overdo it the first time you give her a go. And never go on a bender on the stuff or it's bad, bad news.

The element in nutmeg is psychoactive with its

chemical structure being quite like ecstasy, mescaline, amphetamine. You can hallucinate a bunch of ways but one sensation many users report is the feeling you're floating through the air, off the ground and out to space, or even a gentle cruise through the atmosphere if not sub-orbital. Nostradamus used it for his future seeing visions; Malcolm X said it was like smoking four joints—It's in his autobiography, the clerk says.

He's telling me all this with a grin; he's thrilled, wanting to share the excitement with me, imparting this fun and useful knowledge. I'm feeling myself becoming euphoric, all this foreplay as we're holding the pods, as he grates a tad of a sample into his hand, we smell it and then he planes some onto my palm and I follow his lead licking the fresh ground nutmeg, like the vanilla sugar sample. I swear I'm having another placebo effect, this one having me as I'm thinking I'm starting to float, getting stoked about this new discovery of having some good fun. Giddiness is a widely reported sensation, he tells me, as if I'm not already there with this microdose of a couple of tiny licks.

Then he becomes much more serious as we sample a bit more of it. The clerk says, You can feel the psychoactive effects by ingesting only a few grams of it, as few as five grams, but best to go with ten or so to be sure it hits you right. However, I must warn you, he says, intoxication from nutmeg can produce nerve and heart issues like palpitations, you can get dizzy, have anxiety, and of course hallucinations. He was talking like a pharmacist who was counseling a patient on a new experimental drug they had grave reservations about with all the side effects. Sometimes it takes hours to kick in, he says, while the hallucinations and other effects should resolve itself and be out of your system within one day, 24 hours. Make sure you're in a safe space doing it, like acid, as some feel fear and doom.

I can take those side effects, I tell him, as that's kind of the purpose and sounds rather enjoyable. Is that about it then, I grate these pods or nuts up, put it in whatever, sit back and enjoy the ride for Christmas Eve through the Day, the lady and I, I should say, after we start out with some safe, amorous vanilla fun?

Heh, he says, You got it, man. Lots of pleasure, that's about it. Although...one other common occurrence is the gross nausea, violent vomiting, and explosive diarrhea most people experience. Watch out for that, as you wouldn't want the vanilla foreplay to turn into you two fighting over the toilet all day long, not during the holidays.

What the fuck, I think. I'm standing there all hot to trot, horny from the vanilla talk while imagining my own great floating high from the nutmeg, wondering what other potent things I should buy here, but he's already shooing me through the check-out counter.

At the till, I see this sandy sunburst type coloured pieces of stuff coated in crystal-like sugar. The calligraphic sign says it's candied ginger. I ask him, What does this do? He says, Ginger is a sedative and stimulant as well. It also has aphrodisiac properties. It's good for your stomach, too, helping with digestion. The clerk puts the receipt in my bag, hands it to me and says, And it does all that without making you and your girl shit yourselves after floating about. It would help that condition, in fact.

I'm baffled and, to be honest, I'm a bit put off by it all,

quite a bit. Leaving, I take my bag and the clerk cunt grins ear to ear and he says, Have a great day, a very Merry Christmas, and a Happy New Year to you and yours!

And so, I exit the store, now thinking as I hit the sidewalk, do I still go get the eggnog?

# The Tragedies of Olga and Marion, Part I: The Cat's Bacon

"Oh, Olga, I knew he enjoyed the heat—boy oh boy, like this hot sun out here today. Let's sit on that park bench there under those cool elm trees...but who knew the lovable guy could like the heat so very terribly much."

"I tell you, Marion, my mew sits in our south-facing windowsill all afternoon long, just loving that warmth, soaking it right up off the piping hot glass."

"Smokey would...oh, my! Can you imagine, Olga: we named him Smokey? Dear me! Anyways, he'd go outside and find rocks in the garden and around the yard, ones exposed to the hot sun. It was as if he was a lizard in the desert or something, like an iguana sitting on a lit right up and red-hot rock, basking there. In the house, he'd sit under lamps, rubbing right up against the bulbs, or at least as close to them as he could manage. He'd lay down covering up the furnace vents, tufts of his fur blowing away while he slept, grinning there in his daze like he was imitating Marilyn Monroe. That feline would inch himself closer and closer to the fireplace, leaning in on the screen, taking the odd spark off his fur like nothing at all, as if he had armour coated in retardant on or was impervious to fire. I'd have a pot of soup on the stove, or something in the oven, and he'd jump up and curl next to the pot, or down by the oven door, if you'd let him—it seemed nothing short of scorching himself would keep him away from anything of intense warmth."

"Especially your nice ham bone soup, I bet he liked sitting by that. Or, your fine Sunday roast, Marion. Mmm, hmm..."

"Oh, Olga, you said it. He enjoyed a great diversity in types of meat we offered him, too—of course he would. He ate fish like a cat and bones like a dog. Smokey liked his meat; that's like saying the Pope is Catholic. Although, I have to say, his love of meat was...extreme. Fred wanted to get him as a mouser for around the house, to keep the field mice away from the farmyard and most certainly out of our house. After the incident, well, my poor old Fred said, *We wanted a mouser, not a bleeping porker.*"

"Yes, I'm sure your fine husband wasn't cursing then...ha! No, not your Fred; not like my Roy: foul mouth extraordinaire. My kitty just sits there all day, doesn't do nothing—wouldn't even get up to play with a rodent who crawled over him, not my puss-puss. But was Smokey a good mouser, I mean, before the pig?"

"Oh, yes. Most certainly. We've had mouse problems here for years, those mice coming in from the pasture behind the yard, and the grain bins off the fields on the other side. We tried all manners of poison and traps on them, outside but mostly right in the house. Fred snapped those darn Victors on his fingers, so many times—countless. Once he was fixing the dryer, he stepped on one. The copper coil slammed down getting stuck right on his pinky toe so precisely, the nail turned black-looking like he had the plague or a sickly gangrene or something. They never worked, baited up with the finest cheese and peanut butter or whatnot. We tried poison, setting out the poisonous tablets, all strategic-like, yet within only a few days there were useless blue pills scattered all around in our dresser drawers and right throughout the whole house, as if toxic Skittles were thrown about, everywhere. Omnipresent. Incredible. They were playing games with us, like those pesky mice had us on an Easter egg hunt in our own home. So that's when we got sweet Smokey to deal with those critters—he sure did that all right, taking care of those vermin."

"Heh, though he didn't like them mice as much as he liked Fred's pork, I guess? A vermin pest of a rodent can't possibly compare to beautifully marinated tenderloin, belly, shoulder chops, bacon, whatever you're cooking."

"A carnivore like him must love bacon, as that's his innate instinct, his biological core. If only he could've waited a few extra minutes for it...raw or crisp, no problem. But how Fred cooks it is, he sets the oven on bake for a Mercurial five hundred degrees. Then when it hits that high temperature and dings, he puts the bacon tray in—after sprinkling a dash of that nice demerara brown sugar on the strips—then he turns off the oven entirely. The bacon gets this nuclear-like blast, which is immediate. It works well for fish, too—a nice trout with some olive oil and lemon, would be preferable. Anyways, it gets a concussive sort of heat, keeping the pork nice and moist and juicy, while still cooking it properly, and quickly...you know, the bacteria and whatnot, god forbid if they sometimes still have the worms. It's the only way to do it, truth be told, Olga. Safe and delicious bacon for breakfast, or brunch on Sundays."

"It's like jumping into the sun, or like you say, a bomb blast or something. Oh, Marion."

"Right into the fire, exactly—you said it. It couldn't have been more than a second where he timed his leap in, from Fred holding the oven door open and setting the sheet of bacon in, and before he could shut it again. Smokey liked the heat and the meat, a bit too much—much too much. But he bounced right back out. What a good singeing he got, with melted hair, whiskers vaporized, burnt itty bitty paw pads...you name it."

"Oh, such pain for the unlucky fluffball. And the pain for you and Fred, Marion!"

"That's right, the blistering pain for him and the foul smell for us. I had a fresh jug of lemonade sitting there on the counter, so Fred doused Smokey with that, an instant reaction, a reflex. He was a burnt cat, then a charred kitty with a fine coating of sugary citrus. The acid from the lemons must have stung. He just sat there, fried and stunned."

"And sweetened up further, at least a bit. Oh no. He succumbed to the burns and pain then, right away?"

"No, you know, Olga, they actually weren't that bad, not as bad as you would naturally assume they'd be. They were bad, but not horrible—not like napalm in Vietnam bad, nor like radioactive meltdown in Chernobyl bad, or some such. No, poor guy sat there, struggling from the shock of the singeing, meowing and growling some odd and terrifying sick sound from hell, like he was turned into a demon cat. After the lemonade, Fred rushed again with the next decision, as he's long to do, without giving it much thought. This time to help with Smokey's pain. He grabbed some Aspirin and Tylenol from the cupboard, crushed them on the counter, using the handle of a silver butter knife to sort of smash and grind them up. Fred then went to sprinkling the pain killer powder in with a wee baby bit of wet cat food from a can I'd already opened. The flavour in the can was Smokey's favourite so we were mixing the residue in while trying to focus him on that dish, rather than the breakfast bacon and his related deep suffering. However, I did jump in, ripping up some of the bacon to put on top, since that's what he was after all along. Heh, he was howling and looking like he was wanting to run when I opened the oven to get it; but he stayed put. Fred and I tried to comfort Smokey while convincing him to eat it. It took some time for him to calm down and eat, when the sounds went from the sickly growling meow to a whimper, and back to a nervous sort of purr while he ate, ultimately devouring it all right down to licking the bottom of the bowl."

"Well, that all sounds fine, Marion. I don't understand. Why wasn't it all happily ever after then?"

"Oh, Olga—it was a happy ending for the mice, by all means. But Smokey finished the food, licking his lips for the last time, keeling over almost instantly. We still thought it was something from the incident in the oven, as if he'd had a heart attack, maybe pain-related if not from the shock, or some such. Or then we thought maybe it was a heart attack, but it was from all that bacon and all those years of pork products, an awful coincidence—or a terrible tragedy, especially the timing of it, right then and there even if out of nowhere. The good Lord dost smite him over the bacon, or more likely the fat and grease smiting his wee heart."

"That's how my Roy is going to go, for sure. It's actually a bit surprising we still have him around, now that I think about it—him and all that bacon, so many decades worth."

"Same thing with Fred, Olga, let me tell you. But it wasn't any of that stuff with our dear Smokey. You know, whether the pain or the heart, that's what Aspirin and Tylenol is for, isn't it? And so, for his burn or the bacon, it made such obvious sense to us, in the moment. Yet it just turns out that cats don't do drugs—it should have been D.A.R.E. for ole Smokey, and probably B.A.R.E. for the bacon, too. This is your heart on bacon, and this is your brain on drugs. Drugs people take day after day, for weeks and months! That painkiller killed the pain all right, by going right ahead and killing him right dead, our lovely cat, Smokey."

"Oh, my dear heavens! Poor Marion, and Fred! And the ill-fated sweet little pussy cat! Rest in peace, dear Smokey. You chase them mice in the clouds now, forever: tasty angel mice."

"Yes, you know Olga, the mice wouldn't take the poison, so we got Smokey to get the mice, but he took the poison, inadvertent as it was. I'm just glad it wasn't one of those mini blue mouse pills. That frustration, the irony...well, that heartbreak would have probably killed Fred dead, too."

# Cody's Celebrations, Part I:
# Razing Pumpkins

Our little Cody is so excited he'll trick or treat as a black cat and he wants a cat face carved into his pumpkin this Halloween with whiskers and all too and Ronny from next door was growing pumpkins for Halloween with the biggest one going to Cody this year because Ronny grows pumpkins for the neighbour kids each year and Cody being the youngest trick-or-treater now gets the largest one for Halloween this year but some drunk assholes went ripping right through the garden out back behind the fence near the road by the railway there and they went driving right through the pumpkins in their truck and over them with their big wheels wrecking them all and you could hear the engine roar and tires screech then the dirt and pumpkin shells and pulp hitting the fence and tires screech again back on the road and south facing on the edge of the village they were all already a nice ripe bright perfect orange colour and enormous so not one of them isn't now ruined for Halloween this year so we'll have to go to the market or grocer in town and get one for Cody cause he's young still but old enough now to appreciate it and have fun and he wants a cat carved in the pumpkin which we'll do and light the candle within next to the candy bowl there and hope the spirit of the lit cat in that jack-o-lantern pumpkin haunts them to hell and death and pain next time they drive by back there in their truck those smashing pumpkin bastards though Ronny saw the truck already yesterday morning covered in pulp and seeds and mud and crap parked right there all an orange mess everywhere at his garage so he took the shop pumpkin you know from the reception desk out front and he took it outside and said to me he threw it with two hands of thorough force right through the driver's side window breaking it out and onto their seats with the shattered glass all that gunk and even candle wax went onto the dashboard and leather seats and that one there had a cat face on it too.

# Chicken and Other Conveniences

I couldn't believe how soaked we were by the time we'd made it to the store. It was pouring on the walk over, our ball caps and jackets not having protected us one bit from the deluge. We were quite well buzzed if not entirely on our way to becoming a more fulsome quality of drunk, and it being just before two in the a.m., we were also starving. And so, it seemed like a great and natural idea to walk the four or five blocks and get some fried chicken at the 24/7 shop.

It being well past the point of safely driving (even at this late hour, in this small town up north, and in such proximity to the convenience store), we went about walking it, even as we had to splash our way through the invisible puddles in the cratered asphalt of the dark street. On reaching the lit sidewalk under the glowing sheltered awning of the store, we passed a general panhandler and a more specific one asking if he could bum a smoke, each of whom accosted us but in quite a lazy sort of way, neither receiving their desired items of change nor a cigarette, respectively, before we were able to enter, taking refuge in the store.

Walking ahead (Marty in his hiking shoes and me in my old sneakers), it was as if we were stepping forward wearing fully absorbed carwash sponges, proceeding through the door, mini waves rolling out from the epicenters of our feet. Our ball caps were dripping a considerable trickle onto the grimy eggshell industrial lino-tile floor around our shoes. As the water was pouring off our persons, I thought it would probably be good for the floor, the pure wet solvent taking care of the sticky filth about the place.

Marty went right towards the chicken station positioned at the front centre part of the store, conveniently housed by the check-out till, where the image and deep-fried waft would remind those waiting in line to consider one extra purchase. It was filled with pieces of chicken wings scattered across the warm tin as the various battered parts bathed to a crisp in the incubator under the bright heating lamp. One employee was assisting other customers in front of us with their order of a similar genesis of an alcohol-fueled late-night desire for poultry products, while the other clerk crouched down appearing to stock a somewhat clandestine cupboard with cigarettes, arranging existing inventory while adding to it out of a few larger cardboard boxes, looking almost as if he was playing in a pretend fort of a child's.

The staff and clientele were about what I expected as I gave a brief scan of the store, although I couldn't believe how busy it was for two o'clock in the morning, even as presumably the only place in town open at that hour. *But still...* I thought.

"Ooh, this is going to be good," said Marty, smiling and rubbing his palms together as he was eyeing the deep tin tub of questionable chicken parts. "I'm starving, man. We haven't eaten in forever—that pizza was like six or seven hours ago or something. Jeez."

"We could definitely use a bite," I said, not longing for this chicken necessarily, but I could feel my stomach gurgling and growling, and we obviously needed something to work against the recent boozing of the past number of hours.

As we were waiting patiently at the plexiglass-protected trough of fowl, Marty was noticing the inane conversation transpiring at a sloth's pace between the clerk pinching her tongs and the current chicken-purchasing patrons in front of us. I could hear it was about the amount of chicken being ordered, the price of it, and something about a mutual friend the two of them had, which had nothing to do with the immediate order at hand.

With Marty fixated on his chicken, I noticed three girls standing behind us and to the side. At the end of an aisle, they were all smiling and giggling, all wearing yoga pants of a different feminine shade, something around a median of lavender. The girl in the middle was subtly blushing as they all looked in our direction. They were each sipping away on their recently poured slushies of assorted artificial rainbow hues of fluorescence. The slightly plump girl on the left held a large bag of red Twizzlers, having already shared a stick with each friend, as the blushing girl in the middle, who they were teasing, was twisting the end of it with her fingers while seemingly doing the same on the other end but twirling it around with her exposed tongue in her half open mouth, as if she was performing some oral trick.

I barely had time to look away, which I was wont to do, when the heretofore middle girl (whom I incorrectly perceived to be shy) walked right up to Marty, her slushy still in one hand and the damp piece of licorice seductively pulled out through her also cherry red lips as she said to him, "I like your beard." She was standing close, moving in closer with each candied breath.

While she meant to arouse him with her red Twizzler antics, I noticed her long, satiny hair looked like black licorice, and I was also immediately impressed with her extroverted and confident candor in her mannerisms. I thought she might have known who Marty was, from when he lived here years ago, but then I realized she couldn't have been more than twenty, so that seemed doubtful based on the age spread. With another quick glance around, I noticed a mix of guys in the store who seemed about her age and demographic, each doing their own thing, but it looked like these three girls were in here solo and not having anything to do with the others, motley or civil as they may have been.

I didn't know if I could handle standing there and taking in all this heavy flirting, as entertaining and brief as it might be, so I went for a browse around the store, as we were still no further ahead at that point on moving forward in the short line to get our chicken.

Whenever I walked into such a store, it evoked a nostalgia for my neighbourhood corner store when I was a kid. I had a similar flashback a couple of weeks ago in the city, as they have this specialty candy store there now, attempting to harken back to even older times with certain bulk items and vintage candy sticks and the like, while the rest of the store has a part-Disney and part-diner feel to it, a bit hokey and contrived as they mish-mash different eras, offering antique toys and other kitschy junk along with the more universal and practical candy for sale. But the modern convenience store and the long-expired local corner store were both so far apart in so many respects, even if only these hints of similarities remained, certain faint parallels.

That said, while I was paused in some sort of chicken-ordering purgatory, along with being stuck watching this strange attempted dalliance, as if we were in a scene somewhere between a high school dance and college meat-market party club, I figured only the box of battered bird had a realistic outcome. But not being ready quite yet, I ventured over to check the candy aisle of the convenience store.

I beelined for it, looking down the aisle of the sundry sugary shitty candy, quickly realizing I'd made a bad mistake. Out of place, my thoughts were racing back to the sweet sugar store in the city with all manners of candy, old and new, domestic and imported. Then I was being jolted back a second time, envisioning my own neighbourhood corner store as a kid, the rows of big kid candy and little kid junk merging into one near the middle, where for a nickel you could buy a gummy coke bottle or blue whale, two pennies for a piece of Bazooka gum out of the round container, larger packaged things for a quarter or more. The most sinister thing imaginable (beyond the nutritional value of all the diabetes-causing, obesity-rendering refined glucose, fructose, sucrose...comatose) was only the Popeye candy stick cigarettes for a quarter or fifty cents a package or whatever they cost back then. As cool as it was in the early grades back there and then, the innocence would have remained in the here and now; a seven-year-old pretending to smoke a cigarette, the pointed red mark on the tip of the white stick to eat at the end with a crunch, the phony fiery ashes of the treat. My first quick scan of the store had deceived me, as there was nothing so innocent as a smoke from Popeye here at this store, in this town, at two in the morning on this day.

The first thing I noticed was a man in a charcoal suit with a loose red paisley-patterned tie, who was leaning down into the rack of shit candy as he was pretending to look for a certain item all the while getting a snort off from a Pixy Stix straw, the placebo effect for him taking hold as a faux cocaine high, becoming a jittery Superman for a brief moment. He was sniffling feverishly with disregard for his appearance, dusting his nose off as a routine event, using his thumb while trying to look as though his actions were natural, even if it was explicitly obvious that he was looking for the blue ones (which I later learned are Maui punch flavour), orange being a distant second favourite variety to go up his nose. Along with his discarded Stix, he was chucking the other flavours on the ground as though they were a poison of a totally other substance, some drug that was not quite his, as if the cherry and grape ones were perhaps laced with fentanyl.

*The fizzy powder of the coloured synthetic sugary mix must have a similar effect on him as blow,* I thought, wondering about his mental state. *It seems absurd and impossible, but who the hell knows. Maybe it does a similar such thing on his brain, just in his head.*

There was another guy who was sitting on the floor at

the far end of the aisle, resting in a cross-legged position on his tight jean shorts. He was leaning against a glass door along the wall of coolers for pop and other sugary drinks at the back of the store. The large fellow sported an ear-to-ear grin like a child, while his eyes were closed as if he were in a Gandhi-like trance, or some other certain bliss. He was eating Fun Dip like a kid on the jade green summer grass in the sunny park, using his stick to scoop out the lime as he was licking his stick more and with greater fervour each time trying to ensure maximum coverage. When he couldn't generate more residue off his stick, he went about shredding the packaging, violently pulling it inside out to thoroughly lick each nanometre to guarantee the lime powder was gone, empty from the pack and into his person. And then he was content to move on to the cherry packet, then ultimately the grape one I assumed, unless his tastes were as discerning as the Pixy Stix coke-head. However, I never found out his order of preference, as I was distracted by the final guy in the candy aisle. This brilliant gem that couldn't be missed, surreal as he was, had entered behind me and just replaced Mr. Pixy Stix in his former position, but on the other side.

I'll call him Lotsa Fizz, as he was staring at the eponymous treat on the rack as though it was meth, his eyes surreptitiously darting around the area in their wide-awake state, his crusted lips highlighting his cracked open mouth, as if he was showcasing the teeth rotting out of his head at some gallery's special exhibit. This pathetic individual, wearing clothes looking like he hadn't taken them off in weeks, was trying to crush the candy with his filthy hand, then fake dropping the long string of packaging on the floor, pretending to pick it up but not before stepping on it to break the synthetic crystals within the package, picking it back up as no one was looking. The sad spectacle became an even greater farce as he was attempting to rip it open to gain the fictitious loot, yet he couldn't get a proper grip on it with his grimy paws, so he went to using the last remnants of the mini saw blade on one of the last semi-normal teeth, to rip the plastic and see the crystal pieces trickle out into his dirty palm. He then went to licking, snorting, playing with his index finger, trying to figure out how to make it work, this meth that it surely was, the quartz squares in the plastic strip pockets of red, orange, and burgundy glimmering candies.

At this point in this present dystopia, my recent visit to the contemporary sweet shop in the city and my nostalgia of the corner store of the past seemed like thoughts from another world or galaxy, some utopian dream-like state that couldn't have ever been real, not here on this earth that we know today.

Deciding to walk back and check on the progress of Marty and his chicken, as I exited the candy aisle I noticed some commotion breaking out near the fountain machine, on the opposite side of the store to the chicken station near the cash register. It looked like one individual of above average proportions was hogging the self-serve slushy station by continuing to slowly pour from each fountain to create a ridiculous level of layers, while the other larger individual was seeing their own patience tested during this gigantic cup-filling exercise. By the time I took a proper look over, the one waiting had pushed the other as to move them out of the way to allow for their own turn at a colossal pour, while the incumbent pushed back, spilling some of the humongous cup of frozen flavours onto the shoes of the impatient one. At that, the impatient one dropped a large bag of Cheezies she'd been cradling in her armpit and swung at the incumbent with a wobbly lead from the free hand. The other large lady knew it was coming so she threw her nearly overfull extra-large cup towards the other and they went toe to toe, swinging in confused stupors until they each slipped in unison on the icy floor, landing on their backsides, respectively, the women writhing on the sticky and Cheezie-covered ground, as if they were sent there by artillery shells, if not by their unbalanced and journeywoman heavyweight blows.

As I walked back towards Marty, the flirty licorice girl had turned from him, blowing him a perverse kiss as she returned towards her friends. We passed one another on our respective walks back.

"Whoa, look at that mess," said Marty, laughing in a nonchalant way suggesting he'd seen many similar sorts of events in the past, perhaps even right here at this specific convenience store, or certainly here in his hometown at the least. "I think they might've KO'd one another, both down for the count. Not surprising. And hey, it's good for you to see some of the local flavour like that while you're in town, finally visiting me up here this summer."

"That's no worse than down the candy aisle," I said, trying not to sound incredulous. "You should take a gander down there. It looks like an alley of junkies in some ghetto. There's a coke-head in there snorting Pixy Stix like blow, and a meth-head trying to use Lotsa Fizz somehow. You've got to walk down skid row there to get a frigging pack of gummy bears, or even just some goddamn bubble gum.

Jesus, Marty."

As I was just about to ask him about his encounter with the toying Twizzler girl, the disheveled couple in front of us finally obtained their greasy box of chicken over the glass shield and headed towards the check-out counter; however, they kept walking right out the door, so I assumed they'd prepaid for their order, or maybe they'd cooked some special deal with this corrupt clerk.

"Hi, there. Yeah, we want to get some wings," said Marty, as the clerk appeared more sentient than she was with the last customers, having asked specifically what we wanted. "But do you have more of those good drum parts? Like in the back or something?"

"Um," said the clerk, now appearing as if she might short out on us from his inane request. "I can check."

"OK, but are they cooked and ready to go?" said Marty, questioning as if to rescind his ask if the change was going to delay things much longer. "I'd like a box of only drums if there's any way you can do that for us? They're quite good, the best parts. But if it doesn't work..."

"I'll check," said the clerk, believing she could deliver on the request. "It'll only be a minute."

"OK, great," said Marty. "If you can count them out, and whatever works between those drums and then the rest in regular wings. We'll go with a supersized box of those guys if we can."

"She looks like she might take more than a minute," I said, as I was unconvinced by her glazed-over look. "You think she even knows what drums are? Anyway, tell me about your new licorice friend there. She likes beards, I hear. She's all hot for your scruff, is she?"

The girl was attractive by any measure, other than her

being in here at this hour sipping a Slurpee with her trashier friends. I was genuinely interested in the process of this approach, as she looked like a regular and sober local college girl, although with the blunt appearance and at this shady venue, she could as well have just been a common street prostitute or something as well.

"Yeah, you heard it. She said she likes my beard," said Marty, stroking his beard, which was more of a lazy unshaven streak than anything. "Can you just wait here for a second on the chicken lady, as I forgot to ask her something else...about my refined lumberjack look."

With that, Marty walked off back to where the girl was, and as he advanced, the two friends of the girl both smiled and walked off themselves, heading back towards the magazine stand where they each took some low-brow publication off the shelf, using them as props as they kept talking to one another behind the open magazines they each held. As I'd been following between the path of the two girls and waiting for the chicken lady to return with nothing but tasty drums behind the counter, I looked over to view the conversation between Marty and the flirty Twizzler beard-loving lady, and they were both gone, having totally disappeared from the store floor in mere seconds.

It was like they'd actually vanished or were now invisible, as I didn't even know where one could go and get lost in this slightly oblong box of a wide open store, something which I assumed was designed as such so the clerks were stationed behind the counter on a minor perch one level above the ground floor and therefore able to see the entire store as unobstructed from that vantage point. And yet, even at that not quite bird's-eye angle, it didn't seem to matter at all, as there were no security measures taking place tonight, no concern for the wounded heavyweight ladies still lying there sopping up their slushies and Cheezie dust on the floor, no concern for the ratty candy connoisseurs making a hell of a mess, and no concern for the friends of the girl with Marty, who were now stuffing the magazines into their handbags and jackets.

*With the chicken-fetching clerk still in the back finding or whipping up some fresh drums on short order, perhaps Marty and the girl are back there with her, Marty being even more selective, precisely choosing each of his premium pieces,* I thought. I was doubting it, although I had no other answers for the mystery of their current whereabouts. *Maybe...*

A greying South Asian fellow came trudging out of the back, rolling along a filthy yellow cleaning bucket while seeming to steer the handle of the mop as though it was a giant oar or even a mast. As he reached the central point of the hullabaloo by the slush machine, he slopped the nasty, wet mop right down on the bullseye of the marmalade pulp immediately between the two fallen contenders, mopping away the mess and even nudging them, repeatedly calling them 'sows' in some thick accent and disgusted voice, as if to shoo them off the floor and out of the vicinity, if not right out of the entire store altogether. I'd had enough of that bizarre hubbub, so I decided to go for another short stroll around the store, hoping that it would be a quick jaunt with Marty and his chicken returning any second.

As I walked along at a slow pace, wanting to keep a good distance from any of these assorted deviants and delinquents, I first noticed the Pixy Stix coke-head again. With the original snowstorm having passed, here he was now, jamming his arms way up into a cooler, grabbing for as many Red Bulls as he could muster, a couple of cans hitting the floor as the cooler door slammed against his arms as he was trying to pull them out. One of the cans landed at such an angle it was pierced and began spraying all around him in a light sprinkler-like mist. As with his nose of perpetual twitching and snuffling, this shower didn't seem to bother him either, all these natural events to him, with only his paranoid eyes darting about like a chameleon on speed could possibly give the game away, although it could be surmised that he couldn't even understand that in his sorry state.

I wanted to avoid the mist of Red Bull, so I left the back row of coolers and went up the aisle of hygiene products. There, the Lotsa Fizz meth-head was sitting by the oral conveniences with a bottle of cool mint Listerine. *Yeah, it's kind of late for mouthwash, you dumb asshole,* I thought, as I considered what a truly great irony this was, him taking good and proper care of his long past and well decayed teeth, a good 90+ percent rotted out already, his lips cracked, gums peeling away. But then what should have been instantly obvious to me was made clear quick enough as he was proceeding to open the cap (presumably he'd just ripped the plastic seal off, getting in the early practice from his false crystal candy packaging) and took not a mere sip of the Listerine but chugged it back as if it was nothing but a light beer at a college kegger party. As I pretended to look around him to not seem to be staring, I noticed on the floor beside him was an aerosol canister of hair spray, directly across the row was an opened bottle of

Aspirin, and behind him further down the aisle was one of those travel packages of convenience store condoms with the cardboard box ripped opened. As I was trying to put those oddball pieces of the strange Lotsa Fizz puzzle together, all the while still feigning as though I was simply shopping and not even noticing him, he fired a good round of hair spray into the Listerine bottle and took another chug. That's when I realized he probably didn't notice me there, this gross meth-head now probably blinding himself. Even so, it was time for me to move along.

Turning back up that row and then down the adjacent one, the Fun Dip man had repositioned himself in the potato chip section (having somehow brought himself along all the remaining Fun Dips from the candy section) and was now eating his candy but using Cool Ranch Doritos to spoon out the lime powder, crunching up each pastel green coated triangle with great delight, still in his state of nirvana. Mr. Pixy Stix, Dr. Lotsa Fizz, Yogi Fun Dip—they all looked like they were living the nihilistic zombie life of squalor to me: not so pleasant.

At this point, seeing all these grotesque images while the liquor was continuing to churn in my empty stomach and coarse through my thinning blood stream, I was feeling beyond nauseous by this stage, when from behind me near the front I heard, "Sir, your chicken is ready."

I turned around. The clerk had finally returned and was standing there holding up the box of chicken wings like a trophy, as proof of success in finding the exquisite drums. As I headed towards the counter, I heard from somewhere behind me and on the opposite side this time, "Hey, wait up, bud."

Marty hurdled something at the back and bent down

briefly in one aisle, disappearing for a quick second. He looked a bit off by the time he caught up to me, which I assumed was from his jogging out of the back area and weaving his way around the various scenes of tumult to avoid throughout the store, obstacles abound.

"Oh, man, I'm starving—so famished," said Marty, panting, sweating, and rubbing his stomach this time. "Let's get this back home and get eating. Noshing time, baby."

As I nodded to Marty in a cool concurrence, the chicken clerk at the counter said, "That's twelve dollars for the large box, I'll ring you in over here," and walked over to the cash register, nearly stumbling over the other clerk who was still crouched down there stocking cigarettes in the same cupboard.

"Incredible," I said, trying to whisper it. "That idiot is still moving the smokes around down there."

Marty chuckled, but he had an uncomfortable look and he started patting himself all over. As he ran his hands up and down and over his various pockets, the flirty Twizzler girl rejoined her magazine thieving friends and they exited the store, all three of them smiling our way, the licorice one blowing another kiss to Marty on her way out. Marty now blushed and smiled back shyly, giving a verbal "good night" to them.

"Man, I forgot my wallet, and I'm out of cash," he said, still checking the same pockets over again as if he might have missed one on his first unsuccessful search. "Shit, sorry bud. Can you pay for this? We'll crack that good bottle of Scotch I have when we get back."

"Ha! Nah, no worries," I said, legitimately fine with that, as he'd been a great host to me so far, right up to ordering the pizza earlier in the night. "Of course, man. I'm hungry, too. Time for some chicken. And what about that girl there, where'd you two disappear to? And hey, did they just walk out of here without paying for their drinks and Twizzlers? Her friends took some magazines, too."

"Will that be everything for you?" said the clerk, with a tone of some bizarre air of officialdom.

"I'll get a pack of Camels," said Marty. "Sorry, is that cool? I'll pay you back at the house."

The incompetent cigarette-stocking clerk redeemed himself by instinctively tossing a pack of Camels up to his colleague. She fumbled the catch, but the package landed right at her fingertips on the counter in any event—an easy recovery, then she scanned the cancer sticks.

"Oh, and these as well," said Marty, as if turning something over that he'd stolen. It was the already opened package of condoms from the floor down the oral care aisle.

"Jesus," I said, stunned. I'd heard stories from Marty and from others who knew him going back to high school and college days here, but I was still a bit shocked to see it in action like that, right there and so expeditiously, so carefree (even if with the latex layer of protection).

"Will *that* be all then?" said the clerk, wanting to wrap it up and get us on our way, hopefully to attend to the random chaos in each aisle and all about the convenience store.

"No," I said, matter-of-factly. "Gum. I'll get this Dentyne, spearmint. I'll 'practice safe breath,' with this spearmint Dentyne Ice here, whatever the hell that is," I said, grabbing and slamming the pack flat down on the counter. "I need to clean my mouth. And I feel like I need a goddamn shower when we get back to your folks' place. But you probably need one first," I said to Marty, giving him a fine smirk.

"Heh," said Marty, blushing again as he kind of sheepishly looked outside through the glass door. "It's still pouring. We'll both get a shower walking home right now, so we're all good."

I gave him a brief look of disgust and rolled my eyes, but then smiled and reverted to my thoughts of how impressed I was at his efforts that were in fact really no effort at all on his part. I pocketed my credit card and the pack of gum. Marty grabbed the bag with the pack of smokes and box of chicken, while quietly dropping the opened and now paid for box of condoms at his feet below the check-out counter, kicking them under a newspaper rack, out of sight. We zipped our jackets, adjusted our ball caps, and headed out into the rain for the walk back.

Under the awning, Marty reiterated how hungry he was, and I cracked a joke about how he had no doubt worked up his appetite in the convenience store. We both had a slight chuckle.

"You should have seen this guy in there," I said, about to relay one of the incidents as we set out through the parking lot, into the rain shower of the dark summer night. "He was digging away like a badger in the candy aisle, going to town on the packs of Fun Dip."

"Yeah," said Marty, interrupting me right out of the gate. "Nothing better than a good fun dip at the sev."

# From Paris Green to London Purple

*France*
*September 25, 1916*

To my Dearest Thomas:

I have no doubt you have been anxiously reading the news at home and closely following our various efforts here in France, those of great success and also otherwise, alas. Rest assured, I am alright at the moment, but there is no telling how long that good fortune will last, as we are facing all manner of obstacles and tools in weaponry of the likes unseen by our men before today. Indeed, we were just pushed back from our line in an inevitable retreat as sad and pathetic as it was, and I have not much time to write to you and Ethel now, with things so uncertain as they appear to be at the present time. As but one example, I submit to you such a gruesome threat specific to our current chaotic situation earlier this week...

We were holding our line with effectiveness, in as well-secured a trench as one would find, like if we were ants marching inside a hill made almost of cement, the tunnel-like walkways being reinforced with those heavy sandbags as they are. With no movement on either side for many days, our men soon became frantic, several turning and scattering about, as if they were a school of cod realizing a white shark was dead ahead of them, mouth agape, hungry teeth sparkling.

The men became perplexed as to a line of smoke emanating from the German trench directly in front us, blowing at us. It billowed towards us, this geometric line from precise points on each end, even if incongruent ripples or squiggles moving along the rope of smoke. The Huns had timed this attack for when the conditions of the wind were absolutely exact, as being off on their preciseness of the direction of the draft could lead to a blowback and be detrimental to fatal for them, essentially suicidal. Presumably when it was determined their correct moment was with them, the line took its form and shape, rolling down the short bluff as if a dam broke, albeit in slower motion, allowing the scene to become more ominous. The movement of the smoke was most similar to that which we viewed two summers past from your orchard, that fire straight across on the west side, burning right down the hill to the shores of Lake Okanagan. The difference was this smoke was not following the fire on the ground as in British Columbia, but quite the opposite. There was some fire near the German trench, but it did not move, other than in sporadic and stationary flickers. The smoke led the way on its own, blowing downhill towards us, hovering forward along the ground. It had a hint of canary yellow, as if the fire was indeed leading it down, yet the cloud had more of a seafoam tint to it than anything, or pear. For a brief few seconds, I envisioned that forest fire in Kelowna as though it was chasing the apple orchard floor, like if it was laced with that Paris Green that you use on all of your insects and rodents out there, burning along the grass, creating this path of a dirty lime green cloud on the move. (I have learned they use it to destroy their sewer rats here in Paris, which might possibly be the genesis of the product name—not quite as pastoral and idyllic as it suggests!)

Even as it was still far out in the distance, it smelled of a kind of mixture of pepper and pineapple, all in one more or less appetizing type of breath. It was not necessarily even unpleasant in the least, almost carrying with it a culinary form of aroma. However, as it advanced, the next more unpleasant whiff was that of a bleach-like chemical substance. You knew it was pure poison, not some peppery pineapple dish. Because of the poor gentlemanly souls who experienced this first at Ypres last year, we had an idea of what it really was and thus we had reasonably ample time to don our gas masks and take cover. All the while, we were trying to prepare for an inevitable German assault coming at us from right behind the cloud from which they had set it off. Gunshots were already being fired from that direction, from behind the advancing cloud, as if the bullets were pushing it closer towards us, while cutting through it, piercing.

Unfortunately, one dutiful corporal manned the lookout binoculars for far too long. He was not able to secure his gas mask in time, as during his hesitation a forceful gust of wind came along at the last second, swarming him, smothering him. Frantically trying to secure the mask, he began coughing, violently hacking in short order. As he continued attempting to save himself, his eyes became irritated, unable to see what he was doing, like a blind man lost. Two men, including a medic, rushed over to assist him, but he was now visibly consumed with the poison having entered his lungs and eyes and other mucous membranes, soon to be gone for, asphyxiated.

As I say, for the most part, we held our line, notwithstanding that four or five men had donned their gas masks and tried to run away from the cloud, presumably believing they could indeed outright outrun the approaching haze. It was a fog of certain discomfort and pain and possibly even death. Perhaps they thought they might at least get far enough away for the breeze and air to dilute the poison to ultimately render it ineffective. On the one hand, these several men had already seen much during their time in France, having grown squirrelly in the trenches of squalor and horror. (If only the gas killed just our rats instead of our men, we would be in great shape!) On the other hand, they did act rationally, knowing what could happen to them if their mask was not correctly fitted on their face and head in short order. That said, the Germans could well have advanced and thus these men deserted their trench-mates keeping the position, so they would need to be dealt with by their superiors in some form, those who were not consumed by the fumes nor shot during their scattering (and embarrassing) retreat.

That was chlorine gas, that attack. We had only recently been briefed by a French senior officer, and trained by an English senior medic, on exactly what these chemical gas attacks were and how to manage them. The

Germans were employing many different weapons including these gases, something that was all but totally unknown here just mere months ago.

For some time, the Huns have been using tear gas, which while not fatal, it will debilitate one through serious irritation of the eyes for a short time, a burning sensation with the eponymous tearing up. That, in itself and via the opaque cloud it makes, is effective enough in creating a significant cover to launch full frontal attacks on our lines, as if their indiscriminate artillery fire (into the smoke, towards us) was not in itself enough.

By far, the most dangerous and terrifying chemical they are using is called phosgene gas. It is especially frightening because you cannot see the gas, it being fully colourless. Further, the scent is even more natural and innocuous, like grass or hay that has recently been cut and sitting out in the sun turning a musty sort of odour, not unlike common farmyard smells from our first homesteads in Manitoba and Assiniboia twenty years ago. Often times, this gas does not take effect right away. Sometimes it takes even more than an entire day to realize the gravity of what has happened. When it does kick in, it offers the same brutal irritants in the eyes and throat, while coughing takes over to the point of clear and torturous suffocation, rather than a paltry and overt choking death. The Germans have been killing and injuring many of our men by firing these clear poisonous gas clouds at our lines from their artillery shells, when the wind does permit.

Their most recent weapon we have discovered is being called mustard gas, also having a connotation with the kitchen. There is a yellowy brownish hue in the cloud like umber, smelling of almost garlic or horseradish at first, just like at Sunday dinner. (Unfortunately, out here on the Somme, the Germans serve it to us solo, without the potatoes and Ethel's lovely roast beef. And Catherine's tasty Yorkshire puddings!) This miasma of ochre, or this earthy look of a clay and light dirt, is not even as close to as fatal as the chlorine or phosgene, but the debilitating effects are obvious in the sizzling of the eyes and the singeing of the lungs, as with the other poisons. The mustard gas sometimes comes with a severe blistering of the skin added on top of the other related concerns of charring. These burned soldiers must be cared for off of the battlefield, so it drains our available resources all around, from men in the trench to nurses further afield here in France, across the Channel, and all the way back there across the pond, back at home.

Chlorine, tear, phosgene, mustard. Who knows what is to come. I suggested to the men that we need to invent a potent homegrown chemical weapon in response, such as to combat this Germanified Paris Green chlorine concoction they are using. Maybe we could ingeniously pattern it along the lines of another one of your similar insecticide killer tools of the apple orchard. And while for these larger types of pests we are dealing with over here on the old continent, we already have a great name for it: London Purple! I am certain the Crown and our loyal allies under the Union Flag throughout the Empire would concur, modifying the chemical to take out these larger pests, thus freeing poor Gaul. We simply must make it the deadliest poisonous killer ever conceived of by man, sending some gaseous cloud of mulberry or amethyst right back at them. And it would be preferable if we can have it smell of some combination of garden beets roasting, a fine claret, and succulent plum pie, to make it most unsuspecting.

All my love to you and William there in Kelowna, Ethel and the kids in Regina, Harry and his family in Alsask, George and his in Sibbald, and the rest of our loving family and friends across Western Canada.

God Save the King!

Yours most sincerely,
Alfred

P.S. Have a safe and successful harvest—I can almost smell your apple pies baking over here! (Three cheers for your award-winning Grimes Goldens and Rhode Island Greenings at the last exhibition in Vancouver!)

P.P.S. Know the direction of the wind when spritzing the trees in your orchard with those chemicals. Please, Thomas, practice safe spraying!

# Not Chocolate Chips

OATS. n.s. [aten, Saxon.] A grain, which in England is generally given to horses, but in Scotland supports the people. (Johnson's Dictionary)

"Well, let's go give it one good shot at that premium price," said Gus, looking at the giant pile while scratching at the mesh on the back of his old cap with vigour. "Can't really afford not to—need the cash. Hear they're short milling quality; might be willing to go up a grade. They know how to blend it all in easy enough."

I headed out, hauling the first load to the mill, as Gus wanted to try and get the premium price. He didn't have a contract and the mill would pay considerably more than any other spot price he'd receive elsewhere, if it was a quality product. But as obvious as that was, the problem was so visibly clear when we were loading the truck, that this was not a quality product. It could be seen in the pile itself and then as he went about shoveling the oats into the tray of the auger as we were loading the truck. The foul stench of mould provided further evidence.

"I don't think the mill's going to take this stuff," I had said to Gus, wanting to be honest even if trying to be a bit gentle about it. "It's been sitting in the swathes too long. It's all teeming with this shit now."

*He's paying me for my service of hauling his loads of grain, so what do I care if the mill rejects it,* I was trying to tell myself. The traders and cleaners at the processing plant would laugh, and I'd laugh with them—silly old Gus.

\*

"These are right full of shit," said Rick, one of the grain graders there, who I'd dealt with on many previous hauls. He was pulling back while clinging to the ladder on the truck, as if it was making him gag, which it most probably was. He took another scoop as a sample, then another. "Each scoop here. There're visible droppings in every single scoop—and mildew! Can't clean this stuff up. Can't blend in a scoop of poop. No point in me cracking the hatch then now is there?"

"No, I don't believe there is," I said. I told the guys at the mill that I told Gus what he should have already well known himself. There was no way that mill was going to accept these oats. They could blend in oats with some weed seeds, various dockage, a touch of mildew or spot of mould or dab of poor moisture...but not the exceedingly high levels in this batch. I well knew that at this facility they clean the oats to get them ready to ship off to General Mills and Quaker. "I said to Gus, no one's interested in shitty Cheerios," I said to Rick and Ron.

"Heh, certainly not. A bit of chaff or straw is OK," said Ron, a trader at the mill who had been there for some time. "But no, our customers down south prefer to buy their oats contaminant-free. That's how they've always liked them. But today it's even more so, as they also like them gluten-free, non-GMO, without chemicals—you know, pesticides and herbicides and the like. Their standard keeps changing, making it more than tough enough as it is, changing the goal posts. So I'm pretty sure they'll also want them shit-free, for their granola. Might not notice in those mushy energy bars. But no. No mice, deer, or any other droppings of the kind. No sir."

*There isn't even any such thing as a GMO oat,* I thought, keeping it to myself though, as I wanted to move on from this futile trip of rejection at the mill. *They don't exist. And there's no gluten in oats either. Stupid.*

"You know, they might look like raisins or chocolate chips for the cookies, prepared right into the raw oats, but I don't think that would work either," said Rick, almost philosophical, as if trying his best to offer a creative solution, even if only as a joke. "Much as I'd like to try and help you out—help Gus out, the good and long-time customer that he is. Mice and whatever other droppings in here—they just ain't chocolate chips, nor raisins. Wouldn't work baked into those fancy cookies the city folks enjoy."

Ron did acknowledge a shortage in good milling quality oats within their catchment zone this harvest, and Rick concurred. However, these oats in this hopper were beyond blending for any milling purposes. "It looks like Gus let some cattle on the field too here, letting them graze or at least pass over the swathes during winter maybe," said Ron, pointing to a third type of waste in the oats, and thus putting a bullet in any chance of second thoughts and a last-second negotiation for these oats. However, Ron did suggest I take them down to the elevator, as they were also in need and could maybe find a market with need of them without going high quality milling. "Blending for a less discriminating food market, maybe in Asia or somewhere, or for horses abroad," he said, musing aloud. I thanked them for their time, apologized on behalf of demented Gus, bid them a good day, and headed back to the bin yard on the farm, about thirty miles to the north...

\*

Gus met me on the farmyard road in before the bins, which is where the humongous heap of oats sat on the side, partially under a tarp. As I slowed down to roll forward into the yard, I was considering how out of place the pile looked on the ground next to the large, modern, steel bins, each packed with more valuable crops which had been harvested in good time. The snow fell early last fall and winter set in too soon, leaving the oats stranded in the field. As spring arrived, the snow melted and the first minute the ground was dry enough for Gus to come along and combine last week, he picked them up, dumping them in this vast pile here on the ground. They were covered in a putrid fungal coating from the winter moisture, but he put a tarp over it anyway to keep them from the recent spring showers, which was correct but also seemed ridiculous at this point. The tarp was now pulled back about halfway, although not quite to the level of the peak of the pyramid, oats sliding down in mini avalanches every minute or so, a mesmerizing, almost hypnotic sight. Before I could even get out of the truck Gus flagged me down, gesturing with his hand in a motion to roll down the driver's door window.

"The mill turned them away, unfortunately," I said, breaking the bad news straight away, as if he didn't already know this was going to be the case.

"The elevator wouldn't take them either?" he said, looking confused.

"No, I only went to the mill, but they said there was no way," I said, trying to explain the failed transaction. "Ron suggested the elevator, but I didn't know if that's what you wanted without the premium price, so I just came back here." I wasn't sure why he expected me to know I should have automatically went to the elevator, and there was no way I could have driven from the mill then to the elevator in the west and now back here to the farm in such a short amount of time.

While I was also confused, the uncertainty of Gus seemed to deepen, his tone becoming more exasperated, as if he was flummoxed with me returning directly to the farm rather than going on to the elevator, even though I had no such commercial instructions from him, beyond trying to get the premium at the mill.

"OK," Gus said, scratching the grimy mesh on his ball cap again. "No, fair enough then. I should have said that. The elevator. They'll find a market abroad or for premium feed for the thoroughbreds or something. They're short oats. Take them on down there then, if you don't mind. Thank you."

I gave Gus a nod and proceeded forward, driving the truck into the bin yard and circling back out the farmyard road, back towards the main concession and then the highway, this time heading west.

\*

The workers at the grain elevator didn't have a much different reaction than from those at the mill. I rolled up the elevator driveway and onto the ramp. I got out and, removing the tarp from the hopper, I watched as the probe went in from above. I jumped back into the cab when a couple of seconds later, as the load in the truck was being probed, two of the employees walked over, and so I hopped back out to meet them.

"That's a bunch of garbage you've got in there," said Keith, smiling as though he knew it to be the case without any analytics coming back from the probe, confirming his own hypothesis. "Old Gus got you hauling his junk again?"

"Yeah," I said, gently kicking some gravel in between us, a bit embarrassed. They had to have known Gus's oats sat out all winter and now he was shopping them around. "I told him the mill wouldn't take these, but he insisted. Then he asked I come down here, too, said you're short oats and could maybe blend it for feed in China or something. I had my doubts all along though."

"Heh. Nah, no one needs oats as much as to take these ones," Wayne said, who I had brought a load of flawless wheat to just two days prior, albeit not from Gus. "They'd probably rather starve than get the hantavirus from their breakfast, E. coli in their cookies. Same reaction you'd get with the equestrian crowd. Christ."

"So you won't give Gus a special basis level on this load, for old time's sake," I said, trying to inject a bit of a laugh into this pathetic situation of hauling around the old man's horrific off-grade grain.

"You might find some sloppy brewer to take some off your hands, down in the city," said Keith, climbing up the truck to take a quick look in the hopper. "Sell a millennial a few of these natural bushels to clean up and use. When they ferment it, all the problems get sorted right up good. Especially if they're making oatmeal stout. But even then, no one like that is going to need all these tonnes of it—way too much to clean on a micro-scale like that. Even then, these are just plain poor-quality oats; that's the bottom line. I can see at least three types of crap in here, plus bleaching."

And so, I took the oats back to Gus.

\*

"The feedlot wouldn't even take them?" said Gus, again meeting me before I could get to the bin yard proper. He was less confused and more enraged on this return trip. "Well that's a giant load of BS, those cocksuckers. Livestock'll eat anything! And there's a goddamn global drought on, a shortage of feed even!"

"Well, no," I said, myself becoming further perplexed, as there was never any talk of going to the feedlot. "The elevator rejected it, so I just brought it back here. I wasn't sure you'd want to sell these as feed today, since we started at the mill looking for that premium earlier."

"You take them on to feedlot alley down there. Try the first one you hit going out east, then the next," said Gus, having taken his hat off to now scratch directly onto his scalp, as if it was helping his thought process, itching to brainstorm. "If the cows don't want them, the pigs certainly will."

Gus was looking at the remainder of the heap of oats in his yard. There were another two Super Bs worth of oats sitting there, with another good few tonnes or more after that—at least a couple hundred bushels, of waste. I agreed with Gus that surely a feedlot would take them, where they could blend it into the rations however they wanted to, quite liberally with forage or whatever. And so, I carried on, not bothering to seek clarification on what would happen if even a feedlot rejected these terrible oats, as I also believed they would ultimately accept them.

*

"We don't want this crap," said Bill. He dismissed it out of hand, not even taking a serious look. I figured the mill or elevator must have called ahead, as some sick joke, letting him know these shitty oats were headed his way and that he shouldn't bother with them. "We've got lots of good quality feed here. Yeah, there's some weed issues in some of the hay, some ergot in the grain. But Gus has literal shit here in these oats of his. We simply can't accept it is all. Might make the animals sick. Can't sell sick livestock. Butchers and grocers wouldn't like that. Consumers would lose their freaking minds. Mad cow disease and all."

Well, now I was legitimately unsure of what to do, as I truly did assume the feedlots would take them after being turned away at the mill and elevator. But it turned out the entire regional market thought these poor-quality oats, with actual feces in them, were in fact pure and total shit, in a way. *Should I take them back to Gus?* I thought, imagining his reaction. *What else can I do with them?*

As I was considering what, if anything, I might do with them, Bill spoke up.

"Torch them," said Bill, in a quite direct matter-of-fact sort of way, even if with a smirk. "Take them to the dump and get rid of them. Drive in there, circle around, crack them hatches, and slowly drive on out. Then light them up—you can, or they will at the dump there, for an extra nominal fee. Gus should've just plowed them over and tried again this year. But what else can you do now?"

Bill was offering this suggestion as though it wasn't the first time he'd given this sage counsel to another farmer or trucker. As if it was so obvious, that there was nothing else to do with these poopy dockage crammed off-grade oats other than set them ablaze at a landfill, an innovative option to be sure. Needing the money myself and having yet to be paid for this delivery, I figured it was prudent to return the load to Gus for his final call—I would elicit an explicit decision from him. Either way, I'd unload them back in his yard from whence they came, or he'd cut me my cheque and I'd go dump them wherever on that one last attempt.

*

"I have no room for them back here, you know that. I've got this pile and no free bin space—I don't even have room for that good malt barley still sitting in the grain cart," said Gus, again confronting me before I could make it to the bin yard, nor make it out of the truck. "Bud, we have to get all them oats out of here. I've got enough bait as it is for several lifetimes. Why didn't you just go to the dump and have them plough them under, or burn them all out there? Look, here's your cheque. Unload that truck then come get the rest of it out of here. Torch them!"

# The Final Out

"Are we going to have time for some celebratory beers tonight or is it all official business for you now?" said Ben, winking and smiling as he looked between his pitcher and the attending scouts in the sold-out, full-house crowd.

"No, we're definitely having a few beers," Michael said, the P. "I'll go say hello and thank them for coming to the game, but no formal business tonight—just the boys celebrating our great season."

"Alright, that's good to hear," said Ben, the C, as he held the ball in his fist, punching it into his glove over and over. Ben looked back towards the next and most likely final batter of the night, with 8 2/3 IP behind them. "Well, what are we going to do with him now? How can we help him avoid the rage this time? We don't want him going bonkers again and spoiling our fine evening ahead."

"Hmm, good point," Michael said. "Give him an easy one to pop up? Or maybe just a straight-up K? I'd hope he'd accept that and move on. He's also got his sweet college deal all lined up, or so I've heard."

"You never know with this goddamn nut," said Ben, as he was becoming more focused. "Why not give him one, then we'll finish the next one? You know, that goofy klutzy guy on deck. Give this nut job a base. Maybe walk him, intentionally or not? You'll still get the win and the no-no. I was going to say bean the prick, but honestly I'd prefer we get going and crack those cold ones."

"Oh, Ben...you're going soft on me, right at the end no less," Michael said, half serious but with a subtle smile. "Not now, man."

As the pitcher and catcher conferred, they looked towards the dugout to see if the coach had any signals, but he was not even looking in their direction, as teammates and team personnel on the bench had mentally checked out, looking like they were also ready to go and party.

"Come on, Mike," said Ben. "Let's have some pops. And look at those ladies we can ask to join us." Talking through his mitt and trying to conceal his face, Ben pivoted and used his eyes to point out Michael's family, girlfriend, and all the other girls, looking to the crowd along the first base line and returning to Michael to confirm his assessment. "We don't really need any more shenanigans now, do we? Let's wrap this up and go home."

"OK, OK," Michael said, knowing he should heed Ben's advice. He nodded and grinned as he viewed the crowd, his father consumed with his bag of sunflower seeds, and his mother and girlfriend having their own pleasant chat, about tonight and beyond. "Give me the signal and we'll get her done then."

"Now you're talking," said Ben, Michael's BFF, beaming as he again pulled his mask over his face and jogged back to home plate.

*

By all accounts, Michael was an absolute and complete natural, in every which way—no matter the methodology, Michael was a sabermetrics literal dream on figurative steroids.

As a baby in the crib, not even a year old, he would lie awake, waiting for a feeding. A soft toy ball was placed between the feet of his teddy bear—the bulky mahogany bear in a red bow tie. Michael would stretch out to grab the plush ball with one hand, then he would throw it out of the crib, through the hanging mobile and clear across the room, hitting the clock on the wall, over and over again.

Once a toddler, outside in the backyard, he could throw a plastic ball over the fence by two, across the yard by three, right up and over the house by four. When his father erected the first tee on that back lawn, Michael took the toy bat, gripping and choking up on it, he walked up to the ball placed so perfectly on the tee, taking his first swing—he never even grazed the tee with that inaugural at bat, no...the bat moved flawlessly and without effort, a young Ted Williams there at bat. He would launch the ball with such perfection, over the mauve spring lilacs and smack into the side of the neighbouring house, cracking off bits of honey-coloured stucco, knocking them down into the bed of fuchsia hollyhocks.

Yes, Michael could hit. As he grew up, the uncanny talent grew with him, as if exponentially. His parents would toss him balls, harder and faster each day. Then they threw him Wiffle balls to try and throw him off—he hit them so cleanly they sailed over the fence, over the house, out of the park, seeming to defy basic physics. But Michael wanted to pitch.

Michael would warm up, game out his aim, throw the ball and hit the tee every time, going further back with each throw—a deadly pinpoint accuracy, he had wicked control by age six.

His fastball gained speed with each pitch, seeing double digit gains in velocity on an annual basis, to the amazement of all and to the terror of opposing hitters. Yet even Michael saw it and understood it at a young age. And so, to be fair, once he was playing in the little leagues, he intentionally threw at reduced speeds and without any movement, junk, or tricks—for if he did not throw with some level of restraint and mercy, he would have tossed a perfect game each outing (all season long) in those early days.

Michael's father (his first and best coach) and all his other coaches saw it so early on, they were not even sure how to channel and foster this incredible talent, as it was beyond them. In his early teens, Michael practiced with teams in the men's leagues, testing his skills all the way up to throwing against college players and semi-pros in their off-seasons. Special coaches were brought in. When they were called, they came; others showed up proactively and at random on their own, wanting to help both Michael and themselves. By the time his final month of high school rolled around, diverse and inventive pitches graced his arsenal, with wicked, devastating results for those swinging at the dish, a mere 60' 6" away.

\*

Michael looked for the sign. Ben called for it, straight down the pipe: fastball.

Michael's fastball left his hand like a rocket at launch—it seemed to keep gaining speed until hitting the glove, mercilessly stinging the catcher's hand. He would adjust his fingers along the seams in any number of ways, the trajectory certain to hit the bullseye without fail. For one deviation, Michael would throw a rising fastball to watch the batter swing low to the ground in a golf-like stroke, where the catcher had to jump to control it. Hitters would swing on the speed, only after the catcher already had it safely ensconced in the smoking mitt, but they would feel the concussion on their trembling hands and heat on their windswept faces until the next AB, and then for hours if not days thereafter.

Michael processed Ben's call for a couple of seconds, still thinking of this beast of a batter who had now charged him three times this season, all the while considering his other options. Michael thought: *One: strike him out straight-up, and cleanly so—the asshole probably walks away with his head down. Two: listen to Ben and walk him, intentional or not—he'd be confused with the anticlimactic walk but couldn't do anything other than take his base. Three: hit the buffoon—he gets the base but most likely charges the mound, and maybe I get tossed for the nasty bean.*

Michael prepared for the pitch. He ignored the sign, throwing a planned wild pitch of a full-bore fastball directly over the batter's head, causing the batter to fall, collapsing into the dirt. The sound and the fury of the ball smacking the backstop silenced the crowd. Michael stood tall, ready for the charge or anything, from the batter and/or his teammates on the visiting bench. The batter sat stunned, getting up to his feet slowly, brushing the dust off his pants, and walking right back up to the plate, taking another practice swing and giving a gentle tap on home plate, completely uncharacteristic of this otherwise general thug.

Ben ran back to the mound for another chat.

"Seriously, Mike, what the hell was that?" said Ben, now troubled at this late stage in the last game. "Why do you need to do this now? Everyone's watching, the season's done, you're all set for the big time, the show, and we've got beers tonight. Move on, OK? Let's get this done."

Michael did not even have a chance to respond, as Ben ran right back to the plate, saying something to the batter as he gave him a friendly pat on the arm. Then Ben squatted back into position with another sign: change-up.

This was a safe call for Ben to make, as it was Michael's slowest pitch, yet it looked so fast. Some batters would get wood on it if only because they could not swing any faster. They would read it as though the pitch was a true fastball and not the deception of the slower change-up, thus hitting it in the process as a pure accident—it was rare getting an actual hit, rather tipping it foul most often. It was clean and down the middle, but off-speed to such a degree that some other marginally better batters also saw the pitch as a fastball, but again not being able to read the change-up, they would swing long before the ball even crossed the plate. Michael's delivery of it was identical to the fastball; he could control the speed at almost half the rate and any velocity in between—the more common result being the same thing: strike one! On this occasion, the batter watched the called strike, perhaps still shaking from the last fastball that put him in the dirt.

At a count of one and one, Michael took the sign from Ben and nodded him back a no. And a no. No. No. Rejected, Ben gave up, this time making a slow walk back to Michael, taking off his mask and waiting for the pitcher to offer *him* something.

"OK, fair enough, Ben," Michael said, offering him an apologetic confession. "I shouldn't have thrown that one. I only wanted to have some good fun with this dumb louse here. Oh well, whatever, never mind. Heh, get it?"

"Jesus, Mike, let's just finish this," said Ben, growing more frustrated and visibly so. "What do you want to throw? How do you want to end this out, this game, this season?"

"Let's strike him out, or let's walk him, or let's see if he can hit anything. I don't even care about the no-no right now. We got enough of them this year. So...hmm...let's mix it up. No two pitches alike. Cool?"

Ben walked back to home plate, this time saying something in apology to the umpire, albeit without the collegial pat on the back.

Back to the one-one count call: slider.

Michael's breaking ball broke hard and bad—the incredible movement, the uncertainty of which way it would go...the dip caused mass confusion at the dish. His sinker sunk with such success, it seemed to drown each batter, as if corkscrewing them into the soil as they swung and melted away on every pitch—they swung high up towards the sky when the ball was hitting the dirt, as the pitch dropped several feet in a flash. The twist of the wrist had to be executed with perfection to hit the strike zone, and when it was just off...for great pitchers such as Michael, they land the pitch outside the strike zone on purpose to have the batter swing beyond where he has a realistic chance of giving it a proper hit, pulling him in while pushing him out, yet when the batter stands clam and watches it: ball.

On two-one, Ben wanted to keep the train running on time, giving a quick call for a: curveball.

Where batters blindly thought they could read the sliders (albeit to a rare success), hitters were less hubristic when it came to the curveball, not believing the ball would end up as framed by the catcher, so rather than swing they just watched the strikes roll in, conceding the K and avoiding further embarrassment by attempting to hit it. Michael's curveball saw the downward dive approach the plate, as if his arm was ten years older and stronger—at his age, with his snap so hard, the top-spin with so much movement and rotation, his elbow, ligaments, tendons, biceps, cartilage should have been shredded, a fierce curveball arm like an overripe avocado shoved through a cheese grater. The pitch intensified gravity, where his fastball fought it. Michael could bite it or backdoor it, with variations galore. Those hapless batters who did swing spun their way back to the dugout in a drunken stupor, as if a human twister in slow motion—an unpleasant and veritable vertigo. The downward movement was so fast, the ball so briefly in the strike zone (it always broke, never hung), Ben often struggled to catch it, opting to simply get in the way of it like a hockey goalie to ensure there would be no errant wild pitches on the scorecard.

Strike two!

The two-two signal: knuckleball.

Michael's knuckler (the unconventional clown pitch, as if his conventions were not already enough) made batters look blind, as though they were swinging away in the dark, like a blindfolded child longing to knock down the levitating hidden donkey full of candy. Hitters looked dizzy, flailing about with a Nerf bat at the most elusive of large white butterflies, trying to read the metaphorical wings and actual stitches coming at them in a fluttering crawl. It appeared to be such a simple and clear swing, then the dip at a perverse angle, a last second breeze forces the impossible change in direction, rendering the swing utterly futile, the batter flummoxed and silly. Michael could throw it (or push it off, a more accurate description) with any combination of fingers, nails, and knuckles dug into the leather. The erratic ball would dance its way towards the plate, leaving batters to walk off, bouncing along in their steps, shaking their heads as if still trying to adjust to the incoming fluttery pitch, having swung and missed by three feet—a visual about as equal for a fan as watching a swing from someone who has just taken their first ever swing, or as if giving a bat to a non-human primate and sending them off of the pine bench out to the on-deck circle with nothing more than a wave for good luck.

If it's up high, let it fly;

If it's down low, let it go.

High it was, so the batter let loose, swinging for dear life at that fluttering knuckleball. While he swung through the zone (reading the pace correctly, if not the impossible dance), it was uncertain whether he might avoid terrible embarrassment on this possible final pitch. The ball then dove towards his bat at the last second, allowing him a coincidental and ever so slight tip of the ball over the head of the home plate ump...foul ball. Still two-two.

Ben gave the signal. No. Signal. No. Signal. No. Ben approached the mound. "This is your last conference," the ump said, yelling at them both to get moving it along so they could get this ball game wrapped up.

"What are you looking for?" said Ben. "This is it, let's get it done."

"I want to lob him now, all pitches," Michael said. "Let's see what he can do with just lobs. It'll be interesting at two-two. Our last bit of fun!"

"Oh, man. Why now?" said Ben, rolling his eyes at Michael, his frustration mounting. "OK, done. I won't even sign, do your moon ball thing. And hope to Christ he doesn't line drive you in the face or something."

This was another trick of Michael's trade—a treat for the opposing players, it was not. He could lob the ball in towards the plate as high up and as slow as could be, and he did it with such confidence that any given hitter became so flustered by all his other junk that the batter could not even hit that: a beer-league slow-pitch moon ball. More than one batter would lose it each year, becoming disgruntled by the unseemly tactic, charging the mound on such a grievous insult; however, Ben (the good catcher on the field, and best friend on and off the grass) always had his back. Or, his front in these unique cases, but back of the batter, that is—Ben would take the hitter down, tackling him before the cross-to-enraged batter could reach the star pitcher and swing a fist at his best friend.

*

# The Final Out

Michael and Ben, the pitcher and catcher, best buds, had now both come to the same conclusion of this game needing to end. The final high school game of Michael's career had now seen him start in front of the entire cast of his family, friends, classmates, and most sentient residents in the small, rural town. They knew he was headed away to a glorious pitching career in the majors, a rare bypassing of the college ball with only a few starts in the minors next year (barring a flawless Grapefruit League stint) and he would make the entire town proud with classic 'local boy does good' stories abound for years to come.

With nearly another 9 IP under his belt, the home team was up 6–0, 2 out, bases unloaded, and so another CGS in the works, not to mention a no-hitter still within reach—the perfect game was botched earlier when a neophyte batter leaned in too far on a breaking ball, making 1B on a HBP in the 3$^{rd}$ I. Viewing this significant effort with the local townsfolk tonight were big league scouts from across the national MLB landscape, the AL and the NL: individuals visible on their arrival here in this quaint prairie town, in a clear instant—the eclectic crowd evident, the diversity in the bleachers all here for the one same reason.

One night only, final show in town!

A damn fine outing, as the sun went down.

But those bright artificial ballpark lights shone down with a profound intensity of illumination for this now one last out.

Ben decided to give the sign anyway, giving a thumbs-up, then pointing his thumb straight up twice, providing the green light for the already heretofore discussed lob:

green means go!

As Michael prepared to pitch, he gave a serious gaze down range at Ben, the batter, the crowd. His demeanor and mannerisms were identical to when he launched the rocket above the head on the first pitch. The crowd hushed, not knowing what was coming next, only the certainty of some ultimate ending. The hitter was back at the dish, positioning himself comfortably with his practice swings, seeming unperturbed.

Michael tossed the lob. The final pitch? For the last out...

\*

It was a harmless play, really—routine, run-of-the-mill. Less than an inch in either direction and it might have been different—it would have been different, with countless possible outcomes. The batter could have: watched a ball, strike looking, swing and miss, foul ball, fly out, ground out, base hit, double, triple, home run, in so many scenarios to achieve any one of those.

This particular batter opted for the glory of the home run off of this specific pitch, from this specific pitcher. This hit, this swinging for the stars, became a clipping of the ball, a chipping of this lob, right out into the heart of no man's land in the infield. Who should give chase, retrieve it, get the out—who should cover whom, for this last play, out number 27, to end this game and season?

The young man at first base was a tad portly, a well-proportioned lad who was brilliant at the plate. *But he's not moving from that first base bag,* Michael thought. *In fairness, where else could the coach have positioned him?*

He couldn't run in the outfield, couldn't jump in the in, nor crouch down to catch. And there was no DH in this HS league. And so, he had to play first base—solitarily standing there and catching the harder work of those others who manned the field, both ins and outs.

The current batter (former often mound-charger) had yet another lob tossed his way, and this time he would not make the same mistake—no foul ball, no pop out. He hit the pitch, this one right on top—he merely topped the ball, doing so with one hell of a grand slam, José Canseco in his prime steroids-pumping years, HR manner of a swing. The choppy rope of a roller-coaster not quite line drive took its first bounce early on, while the ball continued to make its way springing along at a decent speed, hugging the first base line.

The alternative scenarios were many, as with outcomes. The standard play (in any game, but especially this one) would have been for Michael to stay on the mound, hoping his unhurried teammate at first might have made a miraculous play, even if only for him. His first base colleague might have simply taken a couple of steps one way to retrieve the ball, then a couple back, for an easy out at first. *A gold glove for the slow-going,* Michael thought, often. With the lob hit towards the base, would he get the base hit?

For the briefest of milliseconds, Michael knew he should remain where he was. Then he knew that he, the pitcher, must make this latest greatest last play, as the toe of the tortoise was not going to be moving off the bag on this hit. Michael knew the batter and now runner was also slow enough, so if he ran right at that microsecond of a moment when the ball was topped, Michael could get to it and either throw to first, or run it right over himself, adding even further glory to him and insult to injury on the out—a tag with the rag, right at the bag: *On this last pitch, how dare you think you could get a hit off of me, even off of my lob!* Michael thought, sincere even if much too cocky.

Thus, Michael chose to make the play. His own hubris was now running into extra innings, musing as if it was game seven, late October, at Yankee Stadium, one out from a perfect game to win it all, thanks to him: the Holy Grail of baseball.

The ball was hit closer to the first base line than expected, where it slowed with gentle bounces along the grass on the ground, close to the dirt path and line, in proximity to the first base bag itself. The pitcher wished to go for the show play: he figured he could bend down during the all-out sprint towards the ball, bare-handing it, tagging the runner—or toss the ball to first while soaring through the air, if that made more sense, a little extra show for the fans.

The runner was doing a life or death sprint of his own in his special shoes—a different pace and path, but the same destination. The first baseman remained in his perpetual place of non-movement, one toe touching the bag, leaning forward hoping the ball would end up in his glove without expending any effort of his own, willing some supernatural force of magnetism.

But then...

As Michael was about to achieve his goal of collecting and actioning the ball all in one Herculean motion, his toe got caught in a rut, enough to send him off-balance as he began his heroic climb into the ether. Gravity would not help him here—his pitching magic might make scouts question physics, but humble astronauts knew the truth.

At this moment of cosmic determination, all three active players and the hundreds of fans watching were awaiting the result—the desired heroic outcome, even if it was a routine play as seen every night on every field.

The few quick seconds felt like eons. The play was in ultimate slow-motion, from any angle—the first base coach and ump were trying to will it, but they could not speed it up. The stumble made Michael look like one of his own clown pitches, or one of his confused and forsaken batters of woe. The great irony. The runner was in full flight, his mind made up there was no stopping for anything, deserving the rightful hit he was now going to get. The first baseman could not move, not that he would have deviated from the bag in any other event.

The bare-handed grab was a poor, terrible, nasty idea, as Michael was still in motion even if already in hindsight. Unlike his pitch placement, Michael's personal trajectory had him land ball first right in front of the bag—he did not even have time to conceive of dishing it off to his teammate, not that he would have been able to during his awkward vaulting, had he indeed thought of and wanted to. With the ball in his bare hand (his throwing hand), his knuckles first touched then crunched hard into the dirt on the first base path, a foot down the line in front of the base. The first baseman could only watch this close-up train wreck of a play develop—he was in position to take the throw, maybe for an out or maybe not, but it seemed he was no longer part of this play, this drama. The man on first had left the plane, unable to guess whether the play would be a great success or a miserably botched one.

At precisely the same moment, now locked forever in time, the runner looked straight ahead to the horizon in the outfield in this run of his life—the universe was expanding as his world began shrinking. The runner was sprinting, sweating, struggling for breath to make the base, sliding in an unorthodox manner, if necessary. While not common practice (sliding into first, and not exactly a forte of this specific runner), his emotions, physical struggle, and status of the play on the field made the choice for the runner to slide.

With his spiky little tough-as-nails custom cleats (a porcupine's dream, along with studs; these may have once been ball, track, or ice cleats, but now looked like a sick modified hybrid pair made with a blowtorch in some welder's garage), the lob-chipping runner also stumbled on touch-down, crushing, cutting, tearing ever so thoroughly, the throwing hand of the good pitcher, Michael. This second falter and collision caused an off-balance challenge now for the runner, as it had just done for the pitcher, leading to a twist and shout, an upending, his torso heavily crashing down on the rest of Michael's distorted arm, smearing blood over both players' jerseys by the end of the gnarly collision.

The screams of horror on the field and in the stands quickly went silent, followed by crying and other sundry shrieks and wails. The first baseman, first base coach, and first base ump stood still, mouths agape. The runner rolled to the side to attend to his own considerable injuries. And there Michael lay, the future Cy Young winner as a bloodied, twisted Gumby in the soft soil, the cool dirt.

His supraspinatus sawed and shredded.

His rotator ripped up, rode roughshod.

His elbow's elasticity eviscerated.

His fingers fucked.

The gore of the dreadful tragedy was evident from the stands—the action and outcome were like a car crash of destruction and death, on a goat trail meets dirt highway in the middle of the cool rye and Kentucky bluegrass field of nightmares. The hand would never again throw metaphorical butterflies, nor catch real ones. The one in a billion talent, the billion to one freak accident.

Tendons torn; fingers forlorn.

The town doctor stumbled down the bleachers and made his way onto the field. Michael's mother and girlfriend screamed and cried while they followed the good doc. Michael's father sat stunned in his seat, while Michael's coach and teammates stood on the field before those closest to Michael realized they needed to expeditiously jog over to the grisly scene and help him.

Ben was already there on his knees next to his teammate and friend, trying to comfort him while avoiding a physical sickness of his own, squeamish at the sight. Michael looked to Ben, then looked to the flurry on the field around him. He looked to the bleachers, where the scouts were gasping, covering their eyes, already walking to their cars, leaving the park and the town, back to their own teams, parks, and homes, in cities far beyond.

The doctor arrived, opened his medical bag, and began feverishly pulling out various disorganized tools, bottles, and bandages. About to pass out, Michael saw the first base ump turning to walk away and make room for the emergency responders, but not before the ump looked back down to Michael, raising his fist, signaling the out.

It was another W and CGS for Michael.

# Farm Family Affairs

Magpies been at him all day, pecking away.

*

Sent him out to pick rocks. Old homestead field down by the ravine way. Wolves must've gotten there, torn him apart.

*

Maybe something else happened. Like a big heart attack. Or stroke. A brain aneurysm. Then the coyotes went and ate at him. Might be a bear got in there too.

*

Thought at first it might've been a mechanical accident. With the rock picker. Or tractor pulling it along. Doesn't really seem the case much now.

\*

Must've had something go terribly wrong and collapsed. Then the coyotes and bears moved on in. Chewed and bled him out right out there, shredded.

\*

Might've just been fixing equipment. And the wolves got him by surprise like, full pack.

\*

Crows and ravens still out there at him now, nipping about.

# When Elephant Got Dealt
## *A Tale for Children*

As Zebra, Camel, Giraffe, Flamingo, and Lion began to rise and shine with the vivid morning sun, they soon discovered their good friend Elephant had undergone some wicked transmogrification during the night.

"Elephant, what happened?" said Zebra, as he went trotting about back and forth at a quick pace, not taking his eyes off the elephant for even one second.

"What the?" said Camel, screaming in disbelief and hoping to draw the attention of the others.

Giraffe's eyes were bulging as his long neck was swaying to position his head higher as if he was a drone, getting an aerial view of Elephant. "He's smaller, and his trunk and enormous ears are gone. It's as if he's been shrunken down in his own skin," said Giraffe, offering the group an official report from above.

"He still looks pretty big to me, the same elephantine size," said Flamingo, jumping to a flutter so to get an all-encompassing view. "But no, I guess he's been changed—transformed a bit, no question. Quite a bit, the more I see."

As usual, Lion was the last of the animal friends to wake up. "What's all the commotion about?" said Lion, giving a lazy growl with his eyes still half-closed. "It's so early in the morning for these shenanigans of yours."

They each looked to Lion as he stood up and stretched out. The sleepy lion reciprocated the glances, then he followed each of their eyes towards the elephant. They stared at their friend, transfixed by his metamorphosis. Their friend took a short glance back at each of them with a look of disinterest as he continued nibbling away at a leafy branch dangling in front of his still steel grey face.

\*

In his flurry of scampering about, kicking up dust in the process, Zebra got something in his eye. "Wait, what?" said Zebra, blinking his eyes rapidly to try and clear the obstruction creating the blur. "My stripes, they're becoming fainter. They're blending into each other, starting to disappear. Jeez, what's happening to me? And Camel, your humps, they're starting to shrink down."

Camel was continuing to stand still, now looking between Zebra and Elephant as he was trying to locate his own humps; however, and of course, Camel could not see anything of the sort. "I can feel it, oh no," said Camel, his mind racing as he imagined what would become of him. "I'm going to turn into a donkey or a pony or something," he thought, as he was beginning to wet himself.

"We're all changing," said Giraffe, in a high-pitched yell. "What's happening to us? Am I shrinking too? My neck, it feels weaker, and my legs. Oh my god—they're altering us, too."

All the flapping had been ruffling up Flamingo's feathers. "I'm turning into a gull or hen or something," said Flamingo, bawling and shrieking with a feeling of certainty that he was also morphing into something other than his regular flamingo self; his good looks of light fuchsia would soon vanish and they would be no more. "Or a tiny ostrich. Yikes! I won't be able to fly any longer."

"My thick mane," said Lion, now wide awake unlike ever before. "It's falling out, the hairs. I'm becoming a female lion, or a cougar, or worse—yes, I can feel I'm shrinking as well. What if I dwindle down into a lowly house cat?"

Whatever had happened to Elephant overnight was now occurring to each of the other five friends, contracting and whatever other changes were imminent if not already underway. Their friend turned away, walking off a few paces as if to give himself some distance from this disorder, soon finding an exposed root system on the ground he began working at, hoping to scrape it out for a light snack.

\*

As they considered their individual transformations and their collective predicament, they looked to themselves and to one another, watching it happen, whatever these motions were that were transpiring in plain sight. Their grief concerning their modifications was immediate, and it was real.

Zebra was having a full-on nervous breakdown. Camel

was in shock to varying degrees. Giraffe was at peak level of disbelief. Flamingo was having a systemic panic attack of some sort. Lion was boiling between a pure anger and an overheated infuriation.

\*

Crying, each of their brains afire, they all looked back towards Elephant when Monkey swung over, through the trees above, to say hello.

"Hi, gang," said Monkey, smiling down to the group of friends from the branch as he peeled a banana. "What are you all up to this fine morning?" Monkey took a closer and better look down, thinking they all looked sick, noticing their red faces and tears as each of the original five stood in their places, trembling. "Uh oh, who died?" said Monkey, only half joking.

"Monkey, can't you see?" said Zebra, weeping and dashing around. "The demented rulers worked their black magic and turned Elephant into this weird thing."

"His trunk," said Camel, inconsolable as he stood still. "It's totally gone, those creeps took it right off."

"And his big Dumbo ears," said Giraffe, sniffling as his neck swung, tears and snot hitting the ground like miniscule, salty liquid meteorites. "They've shriveled them right up into those petite ears."

"And whatever they did to Elephant during the night, they did it to us as it's starting to take effect now," said Flamingo, blubbering and continuing to check his ruffled feathers, believing any hint of rose was fading to blush, at best. "I'm turning into some other plain, flightless bird—I know I am, I know it."

"My mane is starting to fall out," said Lion, roaring with such a ferocity that suggested he would currently maul anyone else who came near, other than his close friends present. "We're all turning into something else right before our eyes here. Monkey, are you sure you're OK, or have you noticed any changes since you woke up? Maybe you're even just becoming another kind of monkey?"

Monkey observed his severely distraught friends on the ground and peered over to Elephant's home turf. Monkey then looked back to each of the five original friends, taking his time in viewing and considering each animal there in their own place, each looking up to Monkey in turn. Monkey looked back and forth, scratching his monkey head, nibbling his banana, shifting his eyes as if deep in thought and struggling to solve some impossible abstract equation. Monkey's eyes widened suddenly when the epiphany hit him, this revelation on the reasoning of why his friends were so miserable in these pathetic and dejected states.

\*

"You silly, clownish animals down there on the ground," said Monkey, snickering with a strong tone of bafflement as he took another bite of his banana. "You think that's Elephant, that they turned him into that guy there?"

"Monkey," said Zebra, smugly questioning Monkey as if the silly primate still could not grasp the severity of poor Elephant's dire situation. "For goodness' sake, look at what they did to our good friend Elephant. This is no laughing matter."

"Yes," said Camel, remaining stationary but shaking his confused head this round, his first movement in some time. "Look at his trunk, it's gone. He's become a monster. He's hideous. These are far-reaching consequences."

"And his ears, Monkey," said Giraffe, continuing to oscillate as if it was now a centrifugal force that would never again see his neck still. "This is pressing—they shrunk them right down into those tiny, sad things."

"We're all changing into something else now, too," said Flamingo, beyond mystified. "My feathers. This is serious stuff, Monkey, crucial—you're up there eating and sloughing it off as though you're still seeing our old elephant friend there. You're still in shock."

"But he's not there, Monkey," said Lion, roaring loudly in great disappointment at the monkey's apparent lack of concern. "Wake up, Monkey—sober up. We need to work together to figure this out, if it's not already too late to save ourselves somehow, to overcome the profound spell they've cast over us."

\*

Monkey rolled his eyes, chuckled, and took another nonchalant bite of his banana.

"You're right. That doesn't look like our regular elephant friend, Elephant," said Monkey, chewing away methodically. "Because it's not Elephant. It's a gosh darn rhinoceros. Listen, let's keep it simple, we'll call him: Rhino."

"Rhino?" said Zebra.

"A what?" said Camel.

"Why would they change him into that?" said Giraffe.

"My feathers, they've now lost all their pretty pink," said Flamingo.

"Are you part of this conspiracy?" said Lion. "Monkey, you better explain yourself right now."

Monkey pulled down the final bit of peel, took the last bite of banana, and chucked the peel, flinging it backwards over his shoulder to discard it into the trees.

\*

Monkey descended to sit on a lower branch of his tree, while the rhino had returned to the branch of the other tree from earlier, taking one last chew, crunching and pulling it down, breaking the bough off. The loud snap caught the direct attention of the five animals on the ground and the one in the tree.

"Your friend, Elephant...he got traded out of here," said Rhino, speaking in a deep and low voice with a raspy undertone, sounding like a comical mobster and dressed in some mammoth iron grey costume. "You got me in return, your new pal here, Rhino. Pleased to meet you all, I'm sure."

"And I heard they threw in some lemurs with Elephant to get you here," said Monkey, as if he had been fully briefed on the matter, or at least had seen and heard the news of the transaction. "I'm still a bit surprised they did the actual trade during the night, but I guess the bosses upstairs...they must have their reasons."

"I don't understand," said Zebra, his eyes wet from the dust and his sadness, his utter confusion blatant in his look and words. "Why would they trade our friend, Elephant? And traded where—what do you mean?"

"Yeah, why Monkey?" said Camel, in stunned hysterics that were now surpassing those of Zebra. "Where is he? Why would they get rid of Elephant like that?"

"Yeah, why Monkey, why?" said Giraffe, whose stumped words were then identically echoed by Flamingo and Lion, each finishing with a squawk and a roar, respectively.

"Wow, you guys are some pieces of work. And I've got to live with you now. Get yourselves together, come on," said Rhino, trying to talk sense into his delirious new neighbours. "That elephant was way too boring out here. A bygone era. They'd had enough of the peanut games, obsolete. So, they gave him the boot and brought me in here, to replace him. End of story. Deal with it."

The five animal friends on the ground stood in silence, universally confounded and open-mouthed with selective eyes continuing to well up and flow, trying to process this information and comprehend the overall situation, with the old elephant, this new rhino, and themselves. And the monkey.

"It's true. I heard them say they needed to spice up the show a bit," said Monkey, trying to console his terrestrial friends below. "We'll miss Elephant, but he's probably in a really great place, or headed there at least. This is nothing to be all so down about. The situation will work out just fine, you'll see."

"Heh, yeah, real fine," said Rhino, with a snarky response. "Elephant was stuck in the mud. He wasn't getting it done. And so, I'm here—Rhino's here to improve this roster. Let's enjoy it, have some fun! We don't really have any other choice. We're on the same team now, so we've got to give 110%, together."

"What about us? Will they trade us, too?" said Zebra.

"Yeah, will they trade us?" said Camel.

"What about Elephant?" said Giraffe. "Will he get traded back to us one day?"

"My feathers, they're still changing colours," said Flamingo. "The taffy is fading, and now they're starting to fall out."

"Monkey, can Elephant ever get traded back?" said Lion. "Rhino, are we going to get traded, too? What's going to happen with him, and with us?"

"They're not going to trade him back and they're not going to trade you. What would they even get in return for you?" said Rhino, doubtful. "And none of this chatter even matters. No one will give a hoot about any of you very soon. This place is going to be totally nuts once those giant fluffy Chinese skunks show up here. People are going to go wild and crazy for them. Trust me, I've seen it."

"Actually, the more I think about it, it's possible you might get traded," said Monkey, speculating while opening a fresh banana. "They're going to need tons of bamboo in here now. They might trade you for a few truckloads of that stuff."

# The Succession Plan; or, Texas Gates and Rumble Strips

I was struggling to open my eyes with this extreme angle and spectrum of rays searing through the cracked windshield, incubating the truck console to kiln-levels of heat. Wisps of grains and particulate sand dust were blowing in through the open window, churning on my skin, while I was listening to some ruckus of turkey buzzard commotion above—the concurrent mix of unpleasant senses went about instigating my disorienting morning.

The sensory overload and unpleasant drunk-to-hangover transition phase was creating a deep uncertainty on my whereabouts, situation, and time of day.

An empty green bottle sparkled like a giant emerald in the passenger seat, bringing some clarity on the throbbing headache, morning aftertaste of disgust, and acute malaise of familiar symptoms continuing to linger between my head and gut, mental and physical.

Slowly gaining enough leverage to adjust my posture in the seat, brushing sand off my soiled shirt sleeves and bared chest, I was scanning the environment with my blurred peripheral vision and direct sight lines from a half-open window; the location was beginning to reveal itself. A large pile of charred smoking palates fumed on the highest dune a hundred odd feet away—a friendly fire of the night gasping its last few breaths, surrounded by sundry burnt beer cans, second and third fern green bottles, both broken and cauterizing atop the expiring bonfire.

The sun was so high in this late summer sky of pure and too perfect azure, it meant it was about mid-morning, give or take, generally thereabouts.

The door wouldn't budge: my lever was rendered useless, as though it was welded securely shut. I kept trying again and again, giving it one final uneventful blow with my shoulder below the window. Rolling down the window and peering out with my craned neck and head looking down showed the chrome exterior handle with a mound of sand immediately underneath it, washboard and ripple patterns afield, the drop-off cliff towards the road in, isolated farms and ranches beyond.

Forcefully caked in a thick bed of sand, the truck was gradually sinking straight into the sand hill from on top. Another few hours from now (which would have been initiated by another Irish bottle earlier) and I knew I'd have been buried alive in a steel Ford coffin. Even if I were lying in a part open casket, it would have been in a sandy grave way down under, tomb of the unknown rancher.

Anger about the situation was my paramount emotion, stemming from my now thoroughly screwed brand-new

F-150. Dad bought me the truck the spring before, after calving and prior to seeding. I didn't have any sense of real worry regarding true danger, as there was an obvious exit. Ostrich-like, I laid my neck out on the glass as if on a reverse guillotine, determining my safe departure strategy from the truck.

Needing to get moving was another key thought I had, making it back to town to meet with my dad, uncle, brother, and the lawyer this afternoon. The date was circled and starred in the calendar months ago, etched in my head even further back: our final succession planning day was later today, in the sand-free town five odd miles off this barren hill.

Peering around, it didn't look like anything was worth taking with me. There was no water or any liquid to help with the near existential struggle I'd have on the road ahead of me, not even a remedial leftover morning-after beer. I took my keys and what else was already present on me; what remained for the truck was a salvage operation, at best. Rolling the window all the way down, I went to shimmy out, landing just below onto the fresh soft sand layer blown in place overnight.

Jumping as my exposed hands planted in the scorched sand flicked my burn reflex switch onto the highest level, I sat back down on my safer Wranglers, blowing my hands cool as if they were a bowl of still boiling soup. Sitting there as I was reflecting on the disappearing truck, I was stared down by the arrogant mangy vulture scratching the rooftop paint with its talons, seemingly pushing and weighing it down below, as if wanting to send the new Ford into the core of hell, a sacrificial offering of carrion with wheels to some devilish truck-loving scavenger bird of Dante's, to a circle of sin and fowl below this mountain of sand.

Standing up, turning back and forth to scan the overall landscape, I wondered why and how it was I came to be here, atop this hill. But the mission of returning to town to deal with the essential meeting was remaining absolute top of my mind; when my thoughts wandered, I disciplined myself to expeditiously return to the only key task at hand: getting back to town, without errant deviations.

My first few steps down the hill in an alpine ski-like motion was reminding me of my barefoot days as a kid in the same spot, but my balance and leverage of today were thrown off by my tight cowhide ropers, coupled with the nasty morning-after-the-bottle effect. I blew a tire, hit the sloping sand, rolling four rotations before managing to slow myself to regain a steady enough position to stand at an angle again. Now, this time, I took even quieter and shorter steps down towards the dirt road, running along parallel and leading into and out of this spot on the sand hills, this wild and forsaken ecosystem.

As I got going on my way out, having time to kill on the walk, I thought hard about my way in. *How the hell did I get here? How did this happen—and what time? Where are the others—who else was here? Why would I drive up there in the new truck? I don't remember the fire, or anything. Jesus.*

Signs of the first formal ranch and any sign of life or civilization came about a mile down the narrow and weathered dirt road which led to the sand hills. I made this milestone quicker than I imagined, walking a slower but consistent pace along the withering quackgrass edge of the silty path, sending swarms of grasshoppers springing to flee with each step forward. At the beginning of the wood and barbed wire fence, a couple of dozen cattle contently went about maintaining themselves in their sterile grassland abode and buffet of sagebrush and minor grass or weeds of nourishment in this late stark season, as the cacti thrived. Fence posts halfway towards the gate into this pasture were covered in antlers and horns of those cervids who had crossed the yard over many decades—hundreds of them lined up and down the fence, with complete skulls on top of the tallest ones at the entrance. It was a surreal and incongruous welcome.

I kept moving ahead, where I was viewing dust being kicked up off the road by the rancher's gate, in inconsistent and blurry patterns. As I got closer and closer, it appeared to be a cow initiating the dirty cloud with some frenzy at its hooves. Walking on the other side of the road to give distance to the increasing turmoil and greater plume, it became clear it wasn't a cow—if it was, it was a horribly anorexic bovine, terminally sick or abused to this end.

What was revealing itself was an antelope caught in the Texas gates on entry, struggling to jerk itself free, with a broken leg busted at a grotesque angle through the crack on landing during a failed run and jump—mates of the herd were long gone. The guard would stop the cattle from thinking about leaving, but not the pronghorn from attempting to enter. Crows and magpies were bouncing around nearby within a shrinking radius of the animal, vultures circling overhead in patterns that were becoming lower, coyotes that had sniffed it out could be heard howling in proximity, all about to compete with their feathered scavenger friends and foes for the certain meal.

From a safe distance between the trailer of a farmhouse and the entrance of the Texas gates, the ranch shepherd and collie barked in a unison of panic and harmonious fury at the hellish scene unfolding at the border with the road, either wanting a piece of the action themselves or only wishing it away from them, warding it all off the property.

*More antlers for the fence, no doubt, I thought. Well, the gophers are safe today, maybe.* A red-tailed hawk flew overhead, higher than the scavenger birds and way above the grisly accident. *Well then, maybe not,* I thought.

There was nothing I could do and nothing I really wanted to do, other than throw a few stones at the avian demons, if nothing other than to check my accuracy and briefly pass the time in this couple of hundred feet of a break on the much longer walk back to town, the miles and hours still ahead.

Considering who might be the great winner and hungry loser in those spoils, my reflections turned to the gains available back in town today. I was again weighing the evening before and my now lingering drunkenness preface complete, the main hangover chapter beginning to take some effect during this first mile into my arduous return journey on foot.

The empty glistening bottle of special booze on the seat. I always enjoyed that bottle, or similar type of bottle. I'd put in one ice cube or a tiny splash of water to open it up, sipping it in leisure, nursing an ounce or two in my glass for an hour or more, that pleasant aroma, relaxing bringer of peace to the body and mind after a hard day in the field, the buzz without the resulting evening of a ready to burst bladder and disjointed sleep.

"That goddamn bastard," I said, kicking some dirt up

for good measure, then screaming. "Argh, the worthless piece of shit—I'll bury that asshole!"

I only bought a bottle of the good stuff for myself on a rare birthday, on no time other than some special occasion. I would make it last for months, savouring my purchase. Then it was gone—no more potent elixir till said day of my solipsistic celebration a few years hence. No one bought it for me but me, I was trying to tell myself. *Alas,* I thought. *Or maybe not.*

Thinking about the aroma, taste, and feeling was too much: I hit the ground landing on both knees, threw my hat off into the taller right-of-way quackgrass, puking with violence—three quite productive heaves, two milder ones, and one more dry one. Wiping my mouth with one shirt sleeve and the sweat off my brow with the other, I noticed some grasshoppers had jumped to what they figured was a zone of safety, away from my hat and knees of crushing death as I entered their currently occupied space, but instead dove straight into the unsuspecting, powerful stream of vomit. I grabbed my hat to put back on, adjusting it on my sweating head, which was also sizzling on the other more interior side of my skull. I was appreciating the irony as the bugs tried to wipe away their own mouths and parts, some stuck and unable to jump back out of the acidic whisky-based spew.

Carrying on, my rage grew. I picked up the pace, heading down the hill towards the ferry crossing over the narrow but deep enough river. Dried tire tracks cut through the path to varying degrees then ran into the grass, entering at abstract twisted approaches to flatten it out, heading to the clay river bank for fishing or fighting or fucking, often times with some requisite drinking involved; new tires trucks did the same, only the ruts were of fresh tread in the dust and gravel. In consecutive steps, I stomped on an empty beer can and kicked some broken glass along the road of dusty aggregate.

I walked further down viewing the tracks and water as the boat left the other side, arriving on my side at the same time as I made the shore on foot. The boat looked like it was hanging from the cable, suspended there. No one got off the oxidized amphibious-looking robotic ferry, and there were no cars waiting on this side with me and my grasshoppers. The aging and weathered captain nodded me on, stood waiting for a moment looking back up the hill from where I had come, then proceeded with his mechanical process of returning the ferry back over its thick pewter cable marked by rusty spots of caramel.

I stood across from the ferryman, watching the strong frothy ripples in the water, gazing between the direction of the road going back to the sand hills and the road going the other way back to town. The boatman watched me, as I eyed both sides.

"Where's your truck?" said the boatman, giving a toothless grin with this knowing smile.

"In the shop," I said, matter-of-factly.

"Heh. Some sand-related fixing, right? Yep, I've seen it before. Take solace, it's not just you, son," he said, drawling it out with some methodology, his grin intensifying with each word. His free arm dangling at his side was shaking.

*The gall of this deranged old beggar,* I thought. But I didn't bother offering him anything in response. With no words nor mannerisms, I was trying my best to show that I couldn't even comprehend what he was asking me, as I continued staring into the flow and pattern of the current of the river in the front and the ripple being generated on the back side of the boat. In close view but growing farther away, two muskrats busied themselves near the dock on the side where the boat had launched for this return trip. One muskrat was pulling away at some reeds and driftwood on the shore; the other was working about, perhaps attempting to build something. Floating between the two muskrats was a crushed can.

"Well, better than the river, you can bet on that," said the boatman, speaking even more slowly in his disheveled hair and grimy clothes. "Much less likely to make her out of this here river. I've seen both, many times. Sand beats water. Let me tell you, sand takes time. Water moves quick—the current pulls you down to the muddy floor, where you get stuck then sucked below to the bottom, to live with the crayfish. You chose well with sand, you did— heh heh heh," he said, with such an odd cackle, looking down towards the water with glazed eyes and laughing to himself, viewing the swirling water on the surface of the deepest section near the middle of the rapid flow of the river.

"True enough there, old timer—true enough," I said, offering a subtle grin of my own, trying to avoid an explicit creeped-out and dismissive tone, believing the boatman to be senile and demented, if most likely harmless nonetheless.

After a moment in silence, the ferry made land, the crossing complete. I started trudging up the hill and not a minute later the boat headed back towards the other side, again with no passengers on board nor any waiting across on the more desolate side of the sand hills. *That crazy ancient coot,* I thought. *Dumb boatman wretch, with all his loony sand and water talk. He's been sailing that ship for far too long, making no sense now. Not that he ever did.*

With the boat, river, and valley behind me and out of sight, I walked off to the edge of the first field of crops, where it first met the forbidding river valley terrain now past. As my hangover was incrementally dissipating, fatigue set in—I was sweating and burning even more, my head and heart were pumping and overheating.

I closed my eyes for a moment as I began to take a much needed and relaxing piss when the rattlesnake set off its tail, shaking it away in a ferocious warning, as a violent maraca at almost point-blank range. I snapped out of my brief trance instantly, jumping back in reflex, this emergency reaction of my own. The rattler had been one step in front of me and I'd pissed right on the snake. *That snake's literally pissed off that it got pissed on,* I thought, both the rattle and myself still shaking. A wave of dizziness hit me, wondering for a second if this was all some sick dream. I figured I should have been snapped at and bitten, assuming the rattler must have been asleep, but I could see the serpent had only just started its lunch—a tan kangaroo rat tail hung out of its mouth as the snake was gradually pulling it in with its distended jaws, bringing it through to join the rest of the body, now the bulk of which was making its way barely past the snake's head, moving beneath the skin a quarter of an inch at a time. I went back to the road to have a proper piss, on the range road being an empty dirt trail between the two golden fields of maturing grain: one durum for pasta, one barley for beer.

These cereals reminded me yet again of the crucial challenge of getting back into town to deal with the main business of the day, then I could manage the business of my own soon forthcoming harvest. And hopefully, after today, there would be a better harvest next year, with more land moving my way, more crops, pasture, and cattle, from dad *and* uncle.

Brothers, Chris and I grew up together, horsing around on the playground in town, on the farmyard, out there at those same sand hills—an innocent and soberer version of this morning. We'd grown apart to the point of almost being estranged. That came about based on questionable circumstances and reasoning from high school right through to today, tensions exacerbating for the past two decades. We'd mended fences somewhat in the past few months, initiated by Chris in an odd way and accepted by me being polite.

Facts remained: Chris was a notorious drunkard, lout, sinner, and had a complete host of other bad traits that seemed to thrive in his core, emanating from his essence. He was a poor, awful, useless farmer. This bum wasn't my true brother, I wanted to believe; because of his terrible failings, I liked to assume he was dropped off here, back in a time of dubious processes, in so many respects. That wouldn't have been his own fault, of course, but he couldn't blame all of that on his being a total worthless piece of dung today. But he did, even if implicitly, sometimes; explicitly, other times, when loaded—which was most of the time.

Chris knew what was coming in the imminent transfer of the land. Most of the farmland was going to me. The land must go to the good son, the good and modern farmer, the family man of faith, staying in the family forever, with the rightful predecessor of those ancestors who laboriously broke this land, the homesteaders of the wild west pioneer times. That was happening today, with near certainty, which we both knew. I was accepting it as my destiny and responsibility and all that was right, while the idiot brother would have to accept his home quarter or half-section or whatever the menial parcel was, and he could move on. A few acres of rye and some special value-added on-farm production in the barn should sustain him through his winter stupor.

Since the patching-up of the relationship and during the surging rekindled friendship of the past few weeks, Chris's recent mood and demeanor was different, as he seemed ready to take that fate, smile, deal with it. And good for him.

And it was him, sure as shit.

"That bloody sod," I said, aloud and screaming to myself again as I walked along the grid road. "He gave me the bottle, the rat fink. That dirty clod."

*The drunk had got the non-drunk drunk, the night before the key meeting,* I thought, keeping my considerations on this internal, thinking about how I was going to have to conserve my energy if I was to make it back alive in this heat and on time. *A despicable tactic, although maybe he's not as stupid as he seems—a conniving rat-bag, for sure, but not a total moron after all. An interesting strategy. He bought me the gift bottle, but if I got that drunk, how drunk did Chris get? Or was this his one night of sobriety to pull off his abhorrent stunt? Nah, unlikely.*

The minds of our father and uncle were already made up though and wouldn't change on a dime because of an unexplained absence—this was only an administrative exercise, a formality of signing the legal papers. Unless Chris believed I would indeed die the sandy suffocating death or by any other natural means out there. *Brutal, either way,* I thought.

I kept on walking. The dirt road became gravel right at the cemetery where all our grandparents were buried—the pioneers were getting their hard-earned and peaceful rest; I would do them right. The land weighed on me heavily, again, constantly: sentimental and financial value wrestled for supremacy in and of my mind, believing a positive like and mutual outcome was certain.

Crossing over the steel tracks, wooden ties, and aggregate of the railway line, I tried to move faster, even as utter exhaustion was setting in. Dehydration and heat stroke were nearby, as my neck and cheeks seared to an untouchable glowing red. As a wilting and hallucinating crab once in the waterless zone of sand, a second wind and hope sprung as I could now see not just the grain elevator: there was the whole town itself, quiet and idyllic, shining in the sun, in peace. There was no sweating, burning, puking in this town—only basking.

The gravel road met the paved secondary highway at a 'T' to end the concession. I saved myself a few steps with a precious energy-saving jaunt rounding the corner in the weedy ditch between the road and the grain.

Approaching town, I could hear the rusty merry-go-round creaking in the gentle wind—a grinding screech when a cog became uncomfortable in its oxidized position, the sound rotating between innocent silence and auditory poison as the breeze and mechanism collaborated on the centrifugal trot of the mini horses on the lonely mini-carousel.

Main Street was located past the trees of the playground where Chris and I used to play for endless summer hours—here was Chris's midnight black horse, here was my snow white one, both colours fading into salt and pepper, towards a common weathered grey. *They were horses, but they would have been more fitting as sheep,* I thought. The meeting place itself was in near view, minus some thin obstructing branches and leafy if yellowing leaves of the poplar trees.

The sound of a truck in the distance grew closer before abruptly shattering the noise of the grating children's playground implement by driving over the rumble strips entering the town proper, adjacent to the park. It didn't seem to slow down. As I was walking close to the stop sign, heavy brakes slammed on made the tires screech on the asphalt beside me. Dad was driving his truck with Uncle Duane riding shotgun.

My mind was racing: *They're going to kill me. I missed it—totally blew it. Why weren't they at the meeting place— have I blown the time by that much? They'll ask about the truck. Oh, Christ.*

"Jesus, Rich, you're a mess—where've you been at?" Dad said, an unhappy query. "The lawyer's waiting for us. And where's your truck?"

"Rich, you seen Chris?" said Uncle Duane, the bachelor, with a perplexed look and before I could answer Dad. "You guys were all out drinking last night. Now we can't find him anywhere either."

The flurry of questions came at me full-bore. They were all reasonable and good ones, with uncertain answers to different degrees. As I processed the question on the whereabouts of Chris, a police car popped out, inching its front end ahead from a side street on the other end of town. It was mere blocks away at that second stop sign in town, then it quickly advanced onto the highway and towards us, but destined for further down the road, beyond where we were. The two fellows inside the police car were at the point of passing us when they noticed our assembled group presently standing on the road and parked in the truck, the revving up of the police engine, braking, screeching tires echoed what Dad had just done— the police car screamed past us marking two fresh black parallel lines, then reversing back over to sit adjacent Dad's red half-ton farm truck. I walked around Dad's truck to stand in between the two vehicles.

"Afternoon there, gents," said Elmer, our county sheriff. He gave Dad and Uncle Duane a pleasant smile; he gave me a dirtier look. I was thinking how the sheriff's slow conversational pace was the opposite of his recent vehicle speed. "Say there, Rich. We got a call just now— we're headed out towards the dunes. Rancher drove by, saw a truck up there, buried from a drift last night. Know anything about that now, might you?"

I looked down, kicking a rock in front of me then scraping the bottom of my right boot back and forth, as the guilty child might. Before I could answer, Elmer chimed back in.

"You call if you do, OK?" he said, seeming to not care whether he got an answer either way. "No, we're not so worried about that one in the sand one, actually. But the boatman on the ferry there says a truck just bobbed out of the river at one of his docks, by the landing. Drifted over and he can't move the ferry now. Goddamn truck right in the mud, stuck in the set path, below the cable over the speedy creek. Incredible."

"You fellas mind following us out there for a few minutes to give us an extra hand?" said the sheriff, asking Dad and Uncle Duane in as serious and sincere a tone as he could muster.

"Well, Sheriff, we all got to head to the office there—lawyer's in town today and we need to square away some business with the farm," Dad said, pointing down Main Street towards the office and looking between Uncle Duane and Elmer cheerily as he was attempting to dodge the request. "Our succession plans there for the farmland are ready, the official legal transfer over, as we're getting too high up there, as you can sure see."

"Well, shoot," said Elmer, laughing it off with a raspy chuckle before bringing it back to a more serious tone. "What so-called business do you have to attend to now? Just get Rich here to go in, sign all them forms, throw him the keys and you're done. You're not giving any to Chris for real, are you? Key-riste! I don't believe it. But hey, it's your business, your farm, not mine."

"Right. Well, love to help you out, Sheriff, of course," said Uncle Duane, segueing quickly away from Elmer's response and Dad's original point, trying to seek an answer to at least one of the outstanding mysteries. "But don't know why you'd need us neither, just to haul out a truck or something?"

"Well, I don't know all the facts yet—that's why I'd like your help, you know," said Elmer, stroking his wrinkled chin. "You've got your business here today, understandable to be sure. But there's a chance, maybe fifty-fifty...a quick trip down to the river might save you some paperwork, some legal bills."

Dad and Uncle Duane were looking at each other and to me in bewilderment, then back to Sheriff Elmer, staring at him as if he was some buffoon trying to tell them a nonsensical riddle when their heads were elsewhere.

"Jeez Louise, what I'm trying to say to you boys is, you know," said Elmer, searching for the right terms. "Your succession plan might've...she might've already planned herself out for you."

I looked at Dad and Uncle Duane, each wearing stunned looks as if they were twins, then I looked down to the ground, trying to mask my own expression to those present. I noticed the shuffling of my feet during this conversation had resulted in my unwitting constructing of piles and trails of sand and silt all about and around my boots, standing there on the road.

In that same moment, I realized my hangover was gone.

# Shopping for Lisa, Part II: Strawberry Fields For...Now

*Cause I'm going to Strawberry Fields*
*Nothing is real*
*And nothing to get hung about*
  *- "Strawberry Fields Forever" by The Beatles*

We're on this quite innocent visit to the farmers' market on a pleasant Sunday morning. And all these city people are in hysterics, crying, writhing about. They're dropping like flies, hitting the ground, rolling around wherever they were standing only brief moments ago—the black asphalt row between the tables of vendor wares, the green grass by the meadowy picnic area, the brown dirt in the field of strawberries near the horse-drawn tourist wagon.

It was the absolute funniest thing I've ever seen in my life, no lies; I say that with not a hint of hyperbole. It was also the most surreal thing I've witnessed. It wouldn't even be a contest—never will be.

Everyone running in an absurd panic, wiping themselves off with any still-dry clothes or whatever they could find, dirty Kleenexes from their pockets, peeling off and using their socks pulled inside-out. I must give Lisa credit on this one, as she stood with a resolute calmness, taking the packet of baby wipes from the pouch of Livy's stroller, handing me one before even taking one herself. I needed a dry one though, as I couldn't contain my tears of laughter, a true optical deluge.

I should say, Livy was sound asleep in sweet dreams with the sun cover thing pulled over, so she didn't feel, hear, or see any of this pandemonium, thankfully—as a toddler, I just don't think she'd've found the humour in it quite yet, although who knows with younger kids as far as what's funny and what's not for them.

Some of these yuppies were walking with their eyes closed and arms out trying to find their way, like zombies on the hunt for a cerebral lunch. Or as if they were in an actual danger zone of some kind, a forest of poisonous flora they had to escape from without touching anything on the path out, lest they scorch their skin.

Many were stripping their clothes off, while those believing they weren't blind yet and could still see were helping those who were believing they'd already succumbed to a permanent darkness, like from some crude noxious gas made by mad scientists. That's what too much TV and internet in the city does to you.

But at the beginning, they thought it was water. Oh, man. Plain old H2o.

I have to say, I thought I was going blind as well, but it

was because of all my teardrops from laughing so damn hard. And it felt like I was working myself into a hernia from the self-inflicted stomach pains. Heh, it was way too much, I just about pissed myself, to be honest. Yikes.

The whole time Lisa is giving me this dirty look as she was sort of packing up, organizing our things so we could get out of there before the chaos got any crazier. But she couldn't wipe the smile off my face—I've truly never laughed so hard or so much and if I'm ever down in the dumps down the road, I'm just going to remember the mayhem there that morning and I'll keep smiling till I'm through the dark period, and in fact smile on till I'm gone forever, no question about that.

I wish I would have had enough juice on my phone to film it all, or the foresight to try for a minute or even a few seconds. That scene of turmoil would've gone viral and gotten millions of hits worldwide—billions, maybe.

\*

So Lisa drags me out to this farmers' market—on my golf day. It's that one a few miles west out on the highway, then you go north a bit on the grid. She's been complaining about me watching too much baseball, bitching about the golf, of course. It was just one of those things where I had to bend over and go along, the timing of it all—some other stuff going on as well, the home front and all.

Anyway, we head out there quite early, as she said, We'll be among the first ones. No, we were struggling to find a frigging parking spot, even barely after dawn, at least it felt like. An already crowded road with cars parked along both sides and into the ditches even, we're ambling into the proper lot, I'm zig-zagging the car along this confused angle parking area full of these tall weeds like Amazonian quackgrass or switchgrass or something, finally finding a vacancy sufficient enough at the end of the lot and near the exit onto the road back out again. Worse than going to Costco on Black Friday or Wal-Mart on cheque day or something, I'm telling you.

After setting up Olivia's stroller, we start walking towards the tents and sweet Livy says, I want strawberries, so we've got to focus on that now, naturally.

When we get to the main market zone, the wagon hauling the u-pickers goes off before we can hop aboard. I'm yelling for it to halt. Wait up, I say, but this straw-hat driving cliché of a prick can't hear or pretending not to as he nods, smirking; but the wagon looks full in any event, all those suburban keeners. Now because we miss it, Lisa wants to wander around to shop first, Then we'll go pick strawberries with Livy on the next go, she says. I'm also thinking, where are we going to park the pram, not being able to take that hulking thing on the wagon out to the field.

We're looking at all the fresh produce and crafty type products. Lisa's chatting with some of the vendors. Livy already looks ready for a nap, lying back in the stroller disinterested in this non-strawberry picking part of the excursion. The market sellers keep going on and on touting how their products are organic, pure stuff, all natural, chemical-free, ultra-sustainable, etc. I was kind of getting sick of hearing about it from these smug merchants, so I took a walk behind the tents by the main building, to get some fresh air.

I'm having a dart back there and I see this guy bossing

around some of the farm labourers, as they're moving some small equipment it looks like, the big cheese shouting at them in a terrible broken Spanish then goes storming off. The workers are feverishly scurrying about to move all this shit, in and out of a couple of ratty sheds by the looks of it, a bit hidden. I figure this might be the owner of the whole schtick of an operation here, the bully supervisor who looks greasier than the grunts, I should add—his demeanor I mean, as he's wearing an ugly almost golden pinkish plaid shirt underneath these fresh navy overalls and rather clean looking tan roper boots; the whole ensemble looks too phony, to me at least.

I finish my smoke break and wander over there to check it out, sticking my head into these shacks since the workers had fled the scene on some other urgent chore from the head man. And what do I see? Huge jugs of chemicals they were trying to put away, I'm figuring, to conceal them now that morning market was abuzz. Herbicides, pesticides, insecticides, rodenticides and the like.

Anyway, not really my business, don't even want to be there, so I saunter back to the aisle with all the market vendors to carry on the outing with my girls.

*

These vendors at this market are really something, each one of them a piece of unique work. You wouldn't believe some of the tripe these folks spew.

"Our bees only fly around in organic fields of clover and sunflowers, growing under rainbows, so we know the honey is pure, as their hives are made of sustainable wood..." I have no idea what a sustainable wood hive is.

"One package of four beef burgers here are guaranteed to be from the same cow, a cow that ate a 100% grass-only diet, a fine grass grown without dirty fertilizer, organic seeds, no chemicals..." How'd they keep the weeds away? That cow must have eaten some dandelions or thistles or something, no? Maybe even a bit of the organic clover the bees enjoy so much? Not 100% grass!

"Cheese from a bottle-fed, hand-milked goat, one living in a most comfy lifestyle, the traditional cheese-making way it's supposed to be..." Don't care.

"Organic, shade-grown coffee beans," says the blue-haired barista covered in ink. Have you seen the various tree frog and butterfly images on the packaging? What the fuck do those even mean? Are there that many different standards, they go out inspecting each crop and area, examining production methods, etc.? I doubt that—very much doubt it, it's all a big scam. Good coffee though, this Ethiopian stuff she offered me, the lovely lady, I must admit, hot, to be honest, er, that coffee.

Not hot: The crazy old cat lady from the Simpson's was there selling her delectable cinderblock-like homemade pound cakes and amateurishly hand-painted garden gnomes—a diverse if eclectic product line, each weighing the same, muttering away to herself, maybe her marketing strategy.

"Chickens, their eggs laid after a feeding of quinoa, for a rich mango-coloured yolk, pure healthy..." Blah blah blah. It's enough to hear all of that nonsense alone to make one sick.

But just then I'm running straight into a bratwurst cart, set up in front of the glass-blower's kiosk, so I was still in good spirits at this point, grabbing a bite...

\*

And so, the good folks who made it on the first wagon to pick strawberries are out there, you can see them. They're out there picking away near their wagon in the field, sunny smiles abound. Past and adjacent the strawberry field is a corn crop, as this so-called organic u-pick strawberry patch is in between this regular corn and the row of vendors and their stalls in the main market area.

Listen to this: This buzzing sound starts up in the distance, low and a ways away at first, growing louder and closer within seconds. I'm thinking, it's nothing to do with anything here. Then this small bright yellow plane can be seen flying towards us, descending on its approach. I'm not figuring much of it, but you can't ignore it as it comes in proximity flying right at us it seems, you can't help even thinking maybe it's a terrorist attack—one can't help but think that ever again, with planes moving in on you like that, building or no building.

Then it adjusts its flight angle, all the while still descending, and you can make out that it's only a crop duster flying towards the corn field adjacent the strawberries. Everyone looks a bit surprised, from the noise and how near it is now, so they're staring at this. When the plane's wings tilt and straighten out, and it's clear it's flying over the corn rows, all the market-goers sort of breathe this big sigh of relief that they're not going to be hit by this kamikaze crop duster. I can hear some people around me in the market saying, Oh, it's just irrigating the field, probably because it's so dry and hot out, and that sort of thing. And you can see the strawberry pickers back to conversing on no doubt the same topic of aeronautics and agronomy. Heh, I bet.

At the same time, I see the snake oil salesman who's the owner of this market, the fucker's holding his phony hillbilly straw hat with both hands like he's about to shred it apart the grip is so tight, wide-eyed and nonplussed, watching the small aircraft. All I can think is, this greaseball knows something we don't know.

The plane hits its mark and sure enough out comes the misty spray from its tanks, gently fluttering down onto the corn. This all good and fine and normal farming practice, right? Maybe it is; however, it's not good and fine and normal at this market, at this time, on this morning. Halfway through its drop, right in the middle of the corn field, right next to the centre section of the organic strawberry patch, a strong gust blows from the direction of the corn plants, like a massive freak plough wind. And the strawberry pickers get wet, like flipping soaked.

This blast of wind, downburst or whatever the hell it was, it was so intense that we all felt the mist from it way over in the vendor area, too. It was kind of funny, a warm day, a bit of a refreshing cooling off those in the shopping zone thought, even if we were all in a bit of shock or at least surprise from this blustery shot of droplets, as if we were at the splash park. I'm hearing a few light laughs, some chuckles and smiles across the market, brief as it was. The rejuvenating dew on the strawberries making them twinkle like rubies under the sun.

Well, it's quiet out now with the plane having flown by, taking its noisy engine along with it. The smiles fade and start to disappear when a couple of soccer moms walking the market row near us eating popcorn look at each other and say, concurrent enough to say Jinx or Beer, they say, It doesn't seem like water, sort of dabbing and sniffing their forearms where the vapour settled, even giving it a lick to taste the droplets. One says, It's not water, it's not clear, it's amber, and I think it smells funny, like gasoline or... garlic. The one who lapped up the drop says, It tastes funny too, it's oily and metallic like blood, it tingles on my tongue, as she offers up a disgusted look as further proof it wasn't airplane aqua.

As these lovely ladies are figuring this all out, one of the dirty grunt workers walks by carrying his weed whipper and he's wearing a big container of liquid sloshing around in what was like a backpack, with a hose and nozzle coming out of it like a belt, clearly some chemical. As this labourer carries on about his business, an old hippie gal screams from her honey hut, as loud as you can possibly imagine her voice to be, she yells, It's not water, it's glyphosate!

*

That's what did it: Roundup. This is when the fun really starts up. What she said echoes across the farm in what might have been the speed of light. The ensuing melee was what you'd imagine, that is, if you were in the middle of a nuclear holocaust, the concussive mushroom blast melting people away. Or if you were among the unlucky sitting ducks storming the beaches of Normandy, the Newfies on the Somme, the Aussies at Gallipoli, etc. Pick your battle. The reaction I mean, not the result. The keeners of the patch, they hit the ground, rolling about in the loose dirt and over the soon to be smushed berries as if they were on fire. You could hear the jammy u-pickers yelling, I can't breathe. Call 911. We need ambulances out here. We're at code orange.

People were descending into madness, thinking they've been doused with napalm in Vietnam, drenching themselves with whatever contents of bottles on their persons remained, many running in mud towards the salvation of the irrigation sprinklers in an adjacent vegetable garden, others heading for any hose, tap, or fountain they could find, flooding to protect their mucous membranes. Vendors were shouting, Call poison control, tell them to send all their resources, my organs are burning, whatever biohazard swat teams they've got, bring them.

One chap was trying to commandeer the horse-drawn wagon, as if to somehow rescue people and get them to safety somewhere. Those in the field and in the market began wailing away, on their knees, rubbing their eyes, believing they've gone blind. As I was mentioning, others are peeling their clothes off, running naked back towards their vehicles, stumbling and tripping along the way, innards hemorrhaging, they're thinking. Many were scrubbing their skin so hard it was peeling and even bleeding as they were trying to wipe away the chemical, this broadleaf weed killer, this would-be VX gas. Several sampling shoppers began inducing vomiting, which was becoming contagious, systemic. It was as if they'd consumed too much nutmeg down at Ye Olde Spice Shoppe. No, it was much worse. Individuals screaming, Call my life partner and tell them I said I love them, my forever last words.

\*

It was so funny—a once in a lifetime laugh. They're loving this cool mist that was so refreshing at first on that hot Sunday morning, till they figure out it's glyphosate. The unfortunate timing of the crop duster and the gust—turning the innocent urbanites into poor wretches, like they were going to die of instant cancer, lost in the country—as it's out spraying the Roundup Ready Corn, not quite the fresh organic sweet corn the slimeball proprietor was selling it as.

Speaking of, that huckster was running away from the market back towards his secret sheds as fast as a three to four hundred pound and sixty to seventy-year-old man could go, a new world record for that combined weight class and age, an easy gold medal in that category. Imagine his sponsorship deals for that effort!

Anyway, so all the strawberry u-pickers were perfectly fine, of course, even if they were all thinking they'd had their spacesuits ripped off by aliens after landing on Mars, or they'd sat right down on some gaseous geysers of another world.

I was struggling to contain my laughter as we were leaving, holding it in just enough to say to Lisa, I guess in the end it worked alright that we didn't make it on time to hop aboard that first doomed wagon ride out to the strawberry patch.

# The Tragedies of Olga and Marion, Part II: Pushing Down Dandelions

"I know it's not my fault. It was just a freak thing, even if he was being a bit careless. I'm beyond upset, Marion. My stubborn Roy, he should've known better. But still, I can't help but think I brought it on somehow—I should never have pestered him like I did, going on and on about it."

"Oh, there, there, my poor, dear Olga. I can't even imagine the absolute terror of it all. However, Olga, it's not your fault in any way—you can't be so hard on yourself for his mistake. An accident is all it was, sad and tragic as it is, of course."

"I kept calling him, out the kitchen window then out the door, telling him his supper was ready and it was going to get cold real quick if he didn't come in soon. Oh, look at me, still crying out here as I was in the church—I'm sorry to put you through all this, Marion. I was becoming more upset than concerned, not thinking about his safety at all. And it was only then when I walked right out the side door to peak around and see what in the heavens my Roy was up to out there in the yard. That's when I saw him there. Oh, save me, Lord.

"The site was utter horror, unlike anything you could imagine or dream of, the stuff of pure nightmares. And I'll be having those nightmares about that scene for the rest of my days, Marion, let me tell you. Nightmares, night and day. Roy was laying right underneath the lawn mower, as if he'd positioned himself there with intention.

"My first thought was the terror that he was all cut up under the blades because of where he was. But maybe he was alright and only fixing the blades that got all tangled up in the thick weeds. My initial reaction was that he'd be all bloody from that based on where he was, but also that maybe he just needed some help. As I ran over, I was wondering, for a split second, if he'd tried to pull a prank on me by doing this, laying down there under the lawn mower, using his backside, crushing the grass, flattening those detested dandelions growing in the side lawn. But I knew it was no joke, as he'd know I might drop dead of a heart attack myself seeing him there on his back under that machine—heart failure like your sweet old Smokey. He was wearing his favourite turquoise plaid shirt, so would never want to get that thing all grassy and greasy, on his back in a position like that, not for some joke. My mind was racing, Marion—or ablaze."

"Olga, my dear, sweet old girl. When you got to Roy, you knew he wasn't cut up, but it was serious and he needed some real help?"

"I got there, Marion, running as fast as I could, even being a bit obstructed by my long apron I'd had on while preparing supper for Roy. The roast he treasured, with mashed potatoes—and lots of gravy... I couldn't even budge that big green machine, a giant tractor for the farm it might as well have been. There was a wrench still in his hand in the arm sticking out. His red toolbox was also placed on some grass and those darn dandelions by the porch. And there was a piece of copper pipe, maybe three feet long. It looked like it had rolled on out, stopping between his feet, which were also dangling out in the open, about up to his knees, or perhaps not quite as far."

"Your Roy was fixing the mower, the good handyman that he was, Olga. There were no cuts or anything, only an accident with the pipe coming loose. A quick way to go for Roy, doing what he loved, Olga. It's all so terrible, but it's not the worst way to go. There, there—it'll be alright, my dear."

"There was nothing I could do, the mower was so heavy. Some primitive jack was found crushed underneath, right next to my Roy—the rusty thing crumbled right out under the big machine. And it's my fault, Marion—I did it to him."

"Oh, Olga—we've been over this, enough already. This is not your fault in any way, not at all. You can't be so hard on yourself. It was nothing but a freak accident, a tragedy—like with Smokey, as you said. Let's look forward now."

"It's my fault, it really is. I insisted Roy trade in his electric push mower for a nice new ride-on one. I told him he was getting too old to push that thing through the yard, that he'd work himself into having a stroke or getting zapped or electrocuted or something. And so, he went out and bought the green beast with the lemon-yellow deer, buying it with great reluctance, I might add. That's what did him in, Marion—that's the truth. It wasn't convenient;

it crushed him.

"He only wanted to have a nice walk in the yard, getting some exercise while cutting the grass. And ridding the yard of those bloody dandelions he so despised. Now he's out of town, pushing up daisies."

# Cody's Celebrations, Part II: Violet Hearts

With all the girly pink red and violet lovey-dovey hearts Cody wasn't ever that fussy about Valentine's Day to begin with aside from the chocolate obviously but at kindergarten the other day they had a silly fun little card exchange where all the kids give out cards and get cards and some bring candy small toys and such items to exchange and well Cody was thinking he's giving out better chocolate than he's getting in because I bought a bag of his favourites at the bulk store to hand out believing he'd like to share those with his classmates but he wasn't liking the treats he was receiving so he starts keeping his own gifts back then gets a bit fiery becoming angry at all the white dark and other kinds of chocolate or god forbid candy that wasn't chocolate because milk chocolate is the only sensible thing to eat and thus give as a treat gift on this kind of day so he snaps after getting a card from some poor country kid which had a Cupid with an arrow through a heart on the card and a Reese's Cup probably leftover from Halloween so teacher said Cody grabs a fork sticking it real forceful like into the peanut butter cup just like Cupid with an arrow he figures as he was so angry thinking that's what he should do smashing it down real hard like on the kids' table piercing the treat turning the Cupid heart card of red pink and violet into two shades of brown plus embedding the orange wrapper into the table with the tines like an arrow.

# NOTES

Page 15: A quote from Carl Sagan is taken from his *Cosmos: A Personal Voyage* TV series, Episode 7, 1980 by PBS.

Page 40: Lyrics are quoted from the song "Mosquito" by the Yeah Yeah Yeahs. © 2013 by Interscope Records.

Page 41: A section is quoted from the book *Cuba Handbook* by Baker, Christopher P. Chico: Moon Publications, 1997. 104.

Page 42: Lyrics are quoted from the song "Santeria" by Sublime. © 1996 by MCA Records.

Page 147: A definition is quoted from Samuel Johnson's *A Dictionary of the English Language* published in 1755.

Page 205: Lyrics are quoted from the song "Strawberry Fields Forever" by The Beatles, written by Lennon–McCartney, double-A side, © 1967 by EMI.

# ABOUT ATMOSPHERE PRESS

Atmosphere Press is an independent, full-service publisher for excellent books in all genres and for all audiences. Learn more about what we do at atmospherepress.com

We encourage you to check out some of Atmosphere's latest releases, which are available at Amazon.com and via order from your local bookstore:

*Buildings Without Murders*, a novel by Dan Gutstein
*Katastrophe: The Dramatic Actions of Kat Morgan*,
    a young adult novel by Sylvia M. DeSantis
*SEED: A Jack and Lake Creek Book*, a novel by Chris S
    McGee
*Shining in Infinity*, a novel by Charles McIntyre
*Willie Knows Who Done It*, fiction and poetry by Hans
    Krichels
*Last Dance*, short stories by Nicole Zelniker
*The Fleeing Company*, a novel by Kyle McCurry
*The Testament*, a novel by S. Lee Glick
*On a Lark*, a novel by Sandra Fox Murphy
*Ivory Tower*, a novel by Grant Matthew Jenkins
*Tailgater*, a novel by Graham Guest
*The Quintessents*, a novel by Clem Fiorentino
*GLLU Boy and the One Saving Grace*, a novel by William
    Waxman
*The Devil's in the Details*, short stories by VA Christie
*Chimera in New Orleans*, a novel by Lauren Savoie

# ABOUT THE AUTHOR

R. Conrad Speer lives in Saskatchewan. He holds a postgraduate certificate in creative writing from the University of Edinburgh.